# MURDER IN
# LOCKDOWN

## THE AUDREY MURDERS

## LEONIE MATEER

---

Published in the United States of America

Mystery/Crime/Fiction
Women's Fiction/Crime
04.22.2020

ebook ISBN: 978-0-9987014-8-6
Paperback ISBN: 978-0-9987014–7-9

*To all frontliners who risked
their lives during Covid-19*

# CHAPTER 1

S he knew she was risking everything to return. If recognized, the last three years of her life had been wasted. Three years of creating a new identity, every moment dedicated to altering the way she spoke, looked, and moved. A slight American accent masked her once familiar New Zealand accent. She spoke more softly, lowered her eyes when spoken to. Her hair was now tied back in a ponytail, dark and shiny; gone were her blonde locks and her buxom physique. Audrey was slender, sophisticated, and—she hoped—unrecognizable.

An announcement came over the speaker. "Please return your trays to the upright position, fasten your seatbelt, and return your belongings to the overhead bins or under the seat in front of you. We will be landing shortly."

Auckland city hadn't changed. Streaks of rain ran across the window, matching her mood. She would have preferred to wait a few more years, but when the pandemic hit, she knew the borders would soon close and she had unfinished business to attend to.

Surprisingly, there was very little resistance going through security. She had expected temperature scanning and filling out paperwork disclosing where she had travelled from. Instead, she saw a couple of medical staff standing talking at a booth, and was simply told to go into fourteen days of self-isolation. She was soon out of the airport, on the street, and into a taxi heading north.

Audrey had done her homework. Numerous phone calls to real estate agents in the far north had resulted in a list of unoccupied homes on the market. One in particular interested her: a cottage in Totara North, a historic little township on the shores of Whangaroa Harbor. The owners lived in Auckland and the tenants had vacated a few weeks ago. It was for sale.

A stop at a run-down secondhand car dealership provided Audrey with a nondescript car. She checked the number plate: CTP133. Perfect. Nothing too memorable. She paid cash and gave the name Anna Ward for the last time. Since leaving New Zealand she had lived and traveled as Anna Ward.

Now she was May Audrey Simmons. Audrey smiled. She couldn't resist using her own name again even if she would be known as May.

Before heading north, Audrey had something important to take care of. She listened to Radio New Zealand broadcasts about Covid-19. New Zealand only had a few cases, but the virus was spreading as more and more New Zealanders returned home from overseas. She was one of them.

# CHAPTER 2

Martin Melrose was preparing for lockdown. With only forty-eight hours' notice, there was much to do. He was planning on finally painting his old, run-down bungalow and replacing the rotting boards on the deck. As he unloaded cans of paint, he noticed the locals taking advantage of the last few days of freedom. They were out in their small pleasure boats on the harbor. Martin had lived in Totara North for almost twenty years. Single and retired from years of teaching, he now spent his days in his garden or on his boat.

He heard a car approaching up the driveway. It was a shared driveway and, apart from him, it had hardly been used since the neighboring tenants had moved out. He'd learned the cottage was on the market when he saw the "For Sale" sign at the bottom of the street a few weeks ago. He watched as a small white car pulled into the neighbor's parking area and a well-dressed woman carrying a suitcase walked up the meandering pathway to the cottage at the top of the hill. He was curious. *Who is she?* he wondered. Were the owners returning? He had never met them. The cottage had been rented since he'd moved in next door. *It must be the owner,* he thought. Who else would be moving in? Her face had been partly concealed by her hat. She seemed out of place, too fancy for this area.

Martin was a little apprehensive about being in lockdown. He'd recently finished a long-term relationship which was going nowhere. She was always going to move in—or so she said. She never did. He had given her an ultimatum: move in, or break up. She had chosen to break up. So here he was, heading into four weeks' isolation alone. He wondered if the woman next door was alone. Surely not. A woman like her would have a husband for sure. He would keep an eye out and see if anyone else arrived. Maybe tomorrow he would go over and introduce himself, if she was still alone. Offer his help. He was, after all, a good-looking man. Still fit and virile.

As he packed all his supplies into the shed, he found himself whistling like the old days. Things were looking up. He would pop out to the store and stock up on wine. *I wonder if she drinks white or red? I should get a couple of bottles of champagne just in case,* he decided. He wondered if she had purchased protective gloves for the lockdown. He would share his. He had boxes of them. He smiled to himself. *This lockdown is not going to be so bad after all.*

# CHAPTER 3

Audrey noticed the man as she drove up the steep driveway to the cottage. *Damn!* she cursed to herself. Nosy neighbors were the last thing she needed right now. She avoided his stare and headed for the cottage. It was just as she expected. Perfect. Sitting high on the hill overlooking the small fishing boats with panoramic views across the harbor. She could see St. Paul's Rock in the distance. The gardens were terraced and overgrown. An old concrete water tank sat unused in the backyard. The cottage had been built in the early 1900s. It was charming. She put down her suitcase at the back door and proceeded to look around for the key. She smiled as she found it under a large flowerpot. People who lived out here trusted their neighbors.

The power was still on. She presumed it had been left connected for viewings. There would be no viewings now that lockdown was imminent. As a precaution, she had removed the "For Sale" sign.

The back door opened to a warm glow of native timber that encompassed the heritage interior. The kitchen was still in its original style with a butcher block, an old hearth, and a long wooden table providing a sense of warmth and homeness. An old piano sat in the entry hall. She lifted the lid and tapped a few keys. It needed tuning.

Audrey chose the bedroom overlooking the harbor. It was smaller but more private. She put her suitcase on the bed and began to unpack. She had stopped on the way to pick up a supply of groceries and noticed people were already donning face masks and gloves and customers were spaced six feet apart in the queue. Since she had arrived a few days ago there were new Covid-19 regulations including the sudden announcement today that all of New Zealand would be in complete lockdown in forty-eight hours. She was glad she had shopped on the way. She had purchased enough to last a few days. She would have to risk shopping locally, although she doubted anyone would expect Audrey Wetherby to be wandering free in their neighborhood. Last time she was here she was on the police most-wanted list.

She glanced in the mirror, removing her hat and releasing her ponytail from its constraints. Her dyed dark hair fell below her shoulders. She liked her reflection. It had been worth the money to remove wrinkles and tighten her skin. She looked younger and different somehow. Her trademark bright red lipstick was the only remnant of the past.

The water was cold. She turned on the hot water cylinder and set up her laptop on the kitchen table. TV1 News was broadcasting the latest Covid-19 cases. The numbers were rising by the day. No deaths yet, but based on what was happening worldwide, she knew it was just a matter of time.

Looking out the window, she couldn't see the neighbor's house. If the man became a problem, she would have to take care of him. The thought excited her. It felt good to be back in her old stomping grounds.

# CHAPTER 4

Detective Constable Steve Mason was watching the evening news. Covid-19, often referred to as coronavirus, was on every news channel. Italy and Spain were losing their citizens daily. China was reporting their numbers were diminishing but were now worried about people bringing it in from overseas and causing another outbreak. America was in denial. Donald Trump was worried about the economy and what financial devastation would be caused with a national lockdown. California's governor was announcing a lockdown but only a few counties were taking it seriously. Mason was pleased his country was acting early by announcing a Level 4 lockdown to take place within the next two days.

The police were going to be busy implementing the lockdown. Citizens were allowed to go out for essentials like food, petrol, and pharmacy supplies. A walk around the neighborhood was permitted but no community contact. Social distancing, it was called.

He looked over at Tracy, the love of his life. She was worried. They had only recently moved to a brand-new house overlooking

Cable Bay. Tracy had made it into a home. Their life was good. This new world pandemic had reared its ugly head quickly. He knew he would be exposed to the virus in his everyday job, so he had convinced Tracy to stay with her friend who had just purchased a bed and breakfast lodge in Totara North. The Lodge would be closed during lockdown, she would have company, and he wouldn't have to worry about her.

"Are you packed?" he asked.

"Almost. I just have to collect all my work stuff," she replied.

Mason knew Tracy 's job at the local newspaper was important to her.

"Has the government confirmed your paper will be in lockdown?"

"We hear future publications may only be digital copies." Tracy started to stuff files into her carry bag. "I don't know why the big newspapers are allowed to run print copies and we can't."

"They just want everyone to stay home. Work from home."

"But a lot of our community is older, and many are not computer-savvy," she pointed out.

Mason looked at the time. "I have to go. You be safe and call me often," he said as he kissed her on the back of her neck. "Don't work too hard, and have fun with Keke."

"I will. Take care, Steve."

Tracy watched her husband back the car out of the garage. She wondered how long it would be before she could touch him again. It was safer this way. He would be exposed to the virus on a daily basis. He didn't want to infect her. She would look for local stories on how Covid-19. was affecting the community. Tracy loved her job. She picked up her keys, locked the front door, got into her shiny red car, and drove the thirty minutes to Totara North.

# CHAPTER 5

Martin heard it on the news at noon. The police were looking for all passengers that had been on a flight from Los Angeles a few days ago. Seven passengers had been diagnosed with Covid-19 and they were asking everyone who had been on Flight AIRNZ1 on that day to contact their nearest police station. They were tracking the passengers by their seat numbers, but there were a few passengers they were unable to locate. Martin was annoyed that the government had been so slow in testing all overseas arrivals. Now, finally, they were isolating all overseas passengers for fourteen days rather than just letting passengers wander off to self-isolate.

It was day one of lockdown and his visit last night to the cottage had proven very unsuccessful. Now he was regretting buying all that wine. He had worn his best outfit, even ironed his shirt for the first time since his teaching days. Finding a bottle of Old Spice in the bathroom cupboard, he sprayed it on sparingly and headed out the door.

He knew she was home. He had not seen her leave and her

car was in the carport. He walked around the back and knocked. He waited. Knocked again, this time a little louder in case she was at the other end of the house. He had always liked the cottage and was curious to look inside. He listened for footsteps. Not getting any response, he decided to walk around the front of the cottage and climb the outside stairway to the balcony and front entrance. He noticed the curtains were closed, yet it was still early. Too early for her to be sleeping.

He knocked on the front door and listened. Nothing. *Damn.* The whole day he had been filled with anticipation and even a little bit of hope this encounter would lead to something. But Martin was prepared. He pulled a pen and card out of his pocket and wrote her a note.

*Hi—Martin, your neighbor here.*
*Just stopped by to see if you need anything before lockdown.*
*Thought you might need some extra protective gloves.*
*Just a little welcoming gift.*
*Feel free to call me.*
*I am a bubble of one and if you are in a bubble of one*
*we can keep each other company during lockdown.*
*I am a great cook and have good wine.*
*021 022 046*

Now they both were in lockdown. He would keep an eye out for her. They were allowed to go for a daily walk in the neighborhood. Living just a few yards from the jetty and the water's edge, he presumed he would catch her taking some air. He realized he was becoming obsessed with a woman he had only caught a glimpse of, a woman who was a complete stranger. He needed to get a life. He decided to go outside and do some gardening in the front yard; that way, he could catch her if she wandered outside.

He had noticed the "For Sale" sign had been removed from the road. Had she just purchased the cottage?

# CHAPTER 6

*Damn, bloody, nosy idiot!* Audrey was quick to close the curtains and disappear into her bedroom when she heard his footsteps crunching on the shell pathway. She had expected him to visit. People here were so damn friendly. Neighborly. She was so pleased when she heard the country was going into lockdown. It gave her the precious time she needed.

Audrey had noticed the man was rather good-looking, sexy even. Tall, maybe just over six feet, with a fit physique and nice walk. She always observed the way men walked. He took a lot of convincing she wasn't home; he'd even climbed up the front stairway and tried looking in the windows. She had waited until he was walking up his driveway before she opened the door and read his note. It was rather sweet. She knew the rules: keep safe, keep in your bubble. But two single people could form one bubble. Maybe she would take him up on his invitation. After all, she only had a limited supply of wine, and why not.

. . .

WHEN SHE AWOKE THE NEXT MORNING, IT WAS DAY one of the lockdown. Audrey realized she had a dry cough; it was constant. It was made worse when she heard on the news the plane she had taken from Los Angeles had seven cases of Covid-19 and they were hunting down all the passengers. What were the chances she had the virus? Audrey never caught colds or flus; it would be unlikely she had caught this virus. She would go to bed for the day and get some sleep. Her body was sore. *It must just be jet lag*, she thought as she wandered into the kitchen, made a cup of coffee, and returned to bed.

She had no choice. No one must know her whereabouts. The police had her DNA and she was not taking any chances.

She propped herself up in bed and opened her laptop. She had a lot of research to do before she could put her plan into action. After an hour online, she took some painkillers and closed her eyes. Her mind was overactive, and it took a long time before she finally fell asleep.

# CHAPTER 7

T racy and Keke Green were sipping champagne and watching the evening news. Keke was drowning her sorrows. She had just purchased the business, which had been one of the best BnBs in the area. Now all future bookings had been cancelled due to the virus. She wondered how she would survive if the lockdown lasted for months. She had a mortgage to pay, and with no income she knew she may have to sell. Luckily, she had applied for the Covid-19 self-employment handout from the government. She was surprised to find over $7,000 in her bank account within a few days. Unfortunately, that would not last more than a few weeks. But she was grateful for anything she could get.

Tracy was everything Keke wasn't: successful, married, beautiful, and independent. Keke thought herself rather plain-looking, definitely overweight and bordering on obese. She had jumped at the chance to spend a few weeks with her best friend. They'd first met at a newspaper function a few years ago. Tracy was the top journalist covering local and international news. With Tracy's husband being the local detective constable, she also reported on any crimes in the area. Keke liked listening to Tracy's accounts of her day-to-day work. Especially when they involved crimes. Keke had followed all the murders in the far north for years. She had a particular interest in the Audrey murders. She had read Poppy Bromley's book on the murders that had taken place between 2012 and 2017. The murderer was a local woman called Audrey Wetherby; she had run a couple of bed-and-breakfast-type businesses. This was a reason why Keke had decided to get into the business. She'd admitted to herself she had been obsessing over the woman for years, and was intrigued by how she had managed to disappear after the 2017 murders.

The newsreader was talking about Covid-19. That was pretty much all the news anyone was interested in these days. How many new cases? How many in hospital? How many deaths? They had just had their first death in New Zealand, which was making people nervous. There was mention of a flight from the USA that had arrived a few days ago with seven people onboard now diagnosed with the virus. They were asking any passengers on the flight to get in touch with the authorities. Keke was pleased there was no one in the far north area reported to have the virus. There was a rumor of someone in Whangarei Hospital, but that was almost two hours away.

Keke looked at her friend sitting cross-legged on a chair. Tracy was good company. They had planned to take a walk down to the jetty tomorrow morning to get some fresh air. Tonight, they would drink champagne and get a little sozzled. She took the last sip in her glass and went to collect bottle number two.

# CHAPTER 8

DC Mason downloaded the information of the passengers yet to be contacted in relation to the Air New Zealand flight from Los Angeles. There were only two they had yet to locate. One was a woman who looked like she was in her forties. With dark hair and green eyes, Anna Ward had not been seen since leaving Auckland Airport. Could be anywhere. The other passenger was a man in his seventies. Mason doubted they would be in the far north but would tell his men to keep an eye out anyway. He forwarded on the email to the local stations. They were busy day and night ensuring residents stayed in their homes and only ventured out for essentials. North of Kaitaia the local Maoris had a roadblock to their secluded village. They were afraid of the virus getting into their people, they said. Other areas were doing similar, taking the law into their own hands. There was a phone number people could call to report residents breaking the rules. The line received thousands of calls and it was up to the police to follow the leads. Overall, people were adhering to the rules. Most preferred to stay home where it was safe. Kids were off school, restaurants closed, bars empty, small businesses shut down, and streets deserted.

Mason preferred to stay at the station. The house was empty with Tracy at Keke's. He checked what was going on that was not Covid-19 related. He saw a couple of murders had taken place on the outskirts of Auckland. The local police thought it was gang related. A lot of drug paraphernalia had been scattered around the house.

Rather than head off home he asked the Auckland Airport police station if they had surveillance footage of the passengers leaving the airport on the day of the Air New Zealand flight. *Might as well be useful*, he thought. After a couple of hours of going through the footage he realized it was a waste of time. He downloaded the footage to a memory stick and put it in his drawer.

His mobile buzzed on the desk. It was Tracy and Keke on video, smashed out of their minds. He wished he could separate what was going on from his personal life. He knew they would suffer in the morning. Tracy threw him a drunken kiss. Keke simply giggled and the screen went blank.

Mason shut up the station and headed out into the night. He wasn't tired yet and decided to take a trip to Kaitaia and make sure the locals were not partying into the night. They were a rough crowd out there with little respect for what the virus could do.

# CHAPTER 9

Martin donned his mask and gloves and headed out the door into another continuous day of perfect blue skies. The drought in the far north had lasted for many months. Lawns were burnt to the color of wheat. The once green rolling hills and surrounding farmlands were crisp and dry. Cattle huddled around water troughs. The price of autumn calves had dropped as farmers did not want to take on new stock until rain was forecast.

But Totara North had an advantage. The small seaside village had blue waters, an all-tide boat ramp, and an old wood jetty projecting out into the harbor providing the perfect place to enjoy the magical calm waters and the stunning views.

Martin made his way slowly down the concrete driveway hoping the lady next door was watching him out the window and would be tempted to join him on his walk. His neat khaki shorts and casual shirt had been pressed with the anticipation of what the day would bring.

Keeping six feet apart was not a problem in such an isolated town. Not one person was out and about. It was day three of lockdown and he presumed most people were adhering to the stay-home recommendation. It felt rather eerie walking down the jetty. Boats were anchored and empty. There was no sign of the usual bustle of local fishermen heading out to sea.

Two women appeared around the bend, chatting enthusiastically, obviously enjoying a chance to be outside in the sunshine. As they approached the jetty, they called out a cheery greeting: "Lovely day." He noticed they were not wearing protective wear, which made him feel overly reactive to the situation in his. He removed his face mask and poked it in his pocket. Lesson number one—don't look like a dork!

Martin didn't recognize the women. He knew almost all of the residents and wondered if they were spending their lockdown in one of the holiday houses in the area. One woman was slender and smartly dressed; the other was quite overweight. Martin didn't like overweight women. In fact, Martin was very particular about the type of women he chose to be with. The woman next door was his type.

He checked the time and saw he had been out for almost an hour and realized it was unlikely his neighbor would be rushing down to join him. All dressed up and no one to impress. He might as well go home and watch the midday news.

# CHAPTER 10

Audrey's cough had slowly improved over the past couple of days. She had stayed indoors, avoiding neighbors and watching the news. She was glad she had changed her ID as the police were still looking for two passengers off her flight, her being one of them. She had kept her head down and had worn a hat so hopefully any surveillance video would not expose her. She had thrown away her complete outfit including the suitcase shortly after arriving in Auckland as a precaution.

The man next door was heading slowly down the driveway. He did look rather tempting but she could not afford to screw up now. She selected a book from the bookshelf and decided to venture out into the backyard. It was private and not visible from her neighbor's home. The cottage was quite isolated, with vacant paddocks on all three sides. She stripped down to just her underwear and was enjoying the warm sun when she heard a rustling in the bushes behind her. She grabbed her blouse, covering herself quickly as a bearded man appeared by the old wire fence.

"I didn't know anyone was living here," he said, sounding annoyed. "Who are you?"

"I live here," she said, trying to maneuver the blouse over her head without exposing too much of her body.

The man just stood there ogling at her. Audrey pulled on her shorts and stood to leave.

"You shouldn't sneak up on people," she said.

"I own all the land around the cottage. Been here for over fifty years," he said, as if he owned the whole town. "You are not the owner. I know the owners. Nice people. Have they rented it again?"

He was asking too many questions. Men who asked too many questions were not safe around Audrey. She had a way of dealing with them.

Audrey changed her attitude. "Oh, what is your name?" she asked sweetly. "I'm May, May Simmons. I purchased the cottage just last week from Bruce and Mary. I would invite you in but with us being in lockdown we have to keep our distance." She chuckled.

"Name is Luke Street. I live at the top of the hill behind you." He grunted as he turned and make his way back up the hill.

Audrey watched the man disappear into the distance. She wondered what had made him come to check out the cottage. Had a neighbor called him? She knew in these small towns her presence would be the latest gossip. *Damn the guy next door*, she thought. *He must have talked.*

# CHAPTER 11

L uke Street was worried. He had known Bruce and Mary Sutton for many years. They had purchased the cottage from him over twenty years ago. They would have told him if they had sold or rented out the cottage. He knew it was on the market, but he had not heard it had sold. Yet the sign was gone from the street. He dialed their number and listened while the phone continued to ring. He left a message. He had been leaving messages ever since he'd noticed the lights on in the cottage a few days before. They'd been on the last few nights. He presumed they were letting a friend stay in the cottage, but today, when the woman said she had purchased the cottage and was the new owner, he knew something was up.

As the day went on, he became more and more concerned. Why had they not returned his calls? He decided he would call the police and have them do a wellness check on them. He had to wait on the line for longer than usual. He presumed they were busy with the lockdown. He left a message for the Kaeo police to return his call.

Luke was an angry man. His last two marriages had ended up

with his wives walking out and taking most of his assets with them. All he had left was his old villa on thirty-five acres at the top of the Totara hill, mortgaged to the hilt. He was in the process of subdividing off two ten-acre lots in order to pay his debts. He was almost eighty and his knees felt a hundred years old. Bloody women.

The phone rang. He put down his glass, struggling to get out of his chair in time to answer it before they hung up. It was the Kaeo police.

"Constable Patterson here. You called regarding a wellness check?"

"Yes, got a problem here in Totara North. There is a lady who has moved into a cottage below my property here. She says she is the new owner, but I know the owners. They live in Auckland and I cannot reach them. They would have told me if they sold their cottage. They asked me to keep an eye on it. I'm concerned something has happened to them."

"Maybe they have gone somewhere to stay during lockdown," the constable suggested.

"No, they are in their sixties, never leave Auckland. They don't even come up here. They would be at their home in Remuera. Can you arrange to check on them?"

The policeman wrote down the details and said he would see what he could do.

Luke felt relieved he had done something. He didn't get a good vibe from the lady. Half-naked she was. All prim and proper. He could tell she thought herself better than him.

He made his way back to the chair, topped up his glass of bourbon, and turned on the evening news. It was all about Covid-19; the cases were increasing daily. Then he spotted her. He was sure it was her. They were showing footage of the two missing passengers from the Air New Zealand flight that had seven passengers on the flight confirmed with Covid-19. He fumbled with the control, wound it back, and then paused on a blurry picture of a woman in a black hat pulling a black suitcase. You could only just see a partial profile of her face, but he was sure it was her. He picked up the phone to call the police and then changed his mind. They would think him a stupid old man and maybe would not bother to check on his friends. He would wait until the police called him. Unfortunately, by the time the police had done a wellness check on his friends, it would be too late for old Luke.

# CHAPTER 12

Constable Patterson made a quick call to the Remuera station to request a wellness check. It was not on the top of his list but he thought he would get it off his to-do list so he could concentrate on manning the local downtown area where it would appear teenagers were oblivious to the lockdown rules. They were hanging out in groups on the streets and having booze parties in their homes.

Totara North fell into the Kaeo district and he knew old Luke. He wasn't one for getting involved in other people's business and Patterson could hear the worry in his voice. He was a strange old guy. Lived alone up in his old run-down villa. There had been a few complaints over the years, mostly domestic disturbances. He liked his booze and to beat up women. The Street family had been in the area for over a hundred years. Totara North was a heritage town known for its sawmill, which was now closed and falling to ruin. Shame about that.

It wasn't until the next day he got word a check was done on the Suttons. Apparently, there was a note on the door advising they had gone to stay with relatives during the lockdown. No address or phone number. But the police looked in the windows and the place seemed tidy and undisturbed. The car was missing from the garage, so they figured they had simply decided to have some company during the lockdown period.

Patterson called Luke but got no reply. He left a message on his phone and hoped the old man would be satisfied that all was okay.

The police had shown surveillance footage of the two missing passengers from AirNZ1 to TV1 News in the hope someone would recognize them. He doubted the passengers would be in his area.

# CHAPTER 13

Audrey waited until the old villa was in darkness. She knew the old man lived alone. As always, she had done her research. It had been quite a hike up the steep hill behind the cottage and the two-acre paddock was overgrown with sharp gorse and vicious pampas grass. She could feel the plants pulling and cutting at her black stretch pants and hoodie. She cursed the man for getting involved in her business. She had looked up the past record of the old man and learned he was a brute. If there was one thing Audrey despised, it was a wife-beater.

IT WAS DARK AND SHE HAD ONLY DARED BRING A SMALL torch. It was low on battery and shone a narrow, dim beam. By the time she reached the villa she was out of breath. Sitting in the darkness on a bench in the overgrown garden, she watched as the man wandered from room to room, finally turning out the lights. She waited at least another thirty minutes to make sure he would be in bed.

It would look like a natural death. She figured he must be in his eighties and no one would suspect anything. Due to the four-week lockdown, family and friends wouldn't be dropping by to visit the old man.

Audrey was at her best in a situation like this. She felt calm, organized, focused. Murder was her expertise. She had honed her skill over many years. Every detail was planned and executed to perfection. She avoided violence if she could, preferring to use other, less messy means of assassination. Tonight, she was using a favorite of hers: a combination of GHB and the highly toxic sap of the oleander plant.

She made her way into the kitchen, listening to the snores of the old man in the adjoining bedroom. She found his drink of choice, Jim Beam bourbon. Perfect! She poured the vial into the almost empty bottle. She smiled when she thought about how surprised the man next door would be to know his kind gift of gloves would come in so handy.

The old man looked like a heavy drinker, based on the amount of empty bourbon bottles lying around the place. Days of unwashed dishes cluttered the kitchen bench. She looked at the photos on the mantel. They were old and dusty like the villa. She made her way to the table and noticed a notepad by the phone. He had written the number for the Kaeo police station. Fuck! She would need to be extra careful.

Climbing down the hill to her cottage was just as precarious. She had left a single light burning in the lounge to look like she was home. Lockdown was a good alibi—not that she thought she would need one. Tomorrow she would take a walk to the jetty. She opened a bottle of wine and chose a movie. *The Portrait of a Lady on Fire*. Perfect. Stripping off to change into comfy sweats, she noticed she had cut herself on the pampas grass. A deep red scratch ran down her forearm. It hurt. Fuck!

# CHAPTER 14

Martin had been keeping an eye on his neighbor. It would seem she had no desire to venture outside. He was disappointed she hadn't even called him to say thank you for the gloves. He was beginning to get a touch of cabin fever and headed out the door for his daily walk to the jetty.

He saw her standing on the jetty. The wind was blowing her blouse tight against her body. He could see the shape of her breasts even from a distance. Her dark hair was long and straight. She was wearing a brimmed hat and dark glasses. He knew it was her. It was more instinct than anything else. She was a stranger not known or seen by the locals. He wondered if he was the only person who knew where she lived. As he approached her, she turned her back and walked to the end of the jetty. He followed, keeping his distance, not wanting to intrude but daring to catch her attention.

She stood staring at the blue calm water of the harbor. He made sure he kept the six-foot required distance.

"Beautiful here, isn't it?"

She took a while to reply. Her voice was soft, demure, with a slight accent that he couldn't recognize—Canadian? American?

"Yes, peaceful," she said.

He noticed she didn't turn her head to look at him. Maybe she didn't know he was the one who had left the note on her doorstep. Why would she?

He was about to make conversation when she turned and walked away. He couldn't see her face for the scarf covering her nose and mouth as if to adhere to the virus warnings. He noticed she wasn't wearing gloves.

He turned to follow her, but she was walking so quickly he would have to run to catch her and look really foolish or, worse, like a stalker. By the time he reached the driveway they shared she was already at the cottage. Damn! With lockdown he couldn't just go visit her. He would have to wait to see if she called. He was fascinated with this woman. She was mysterious, sexy, had a great body, and was someone he knew he wanted to get to know.

MAYBE SHE WOULD BE AT THE JETTY TOMORROW. HE hoped so. Back inside, he turned on the afternoon Covid-19 update and saw the numbers were continuing to rise. No new deaths, thank goodness. He hoped the lockdown would eventually get the numbers down. They were showing a video of the missing passengers from the AIRNZ1 flight. He blinked. *Shit! It's her.* He was sure it was her. He paused the screen and stared at the blurred image of a dark-haired woman in a black hat pulling a black suitcase. *No. It can't be,* he thought. The suitcase was different. The hat was different. The woman in the cottage was carrying a bright pink suitcase. He remembered that quite distinctly. He had never seen a suitcase like that before. He also had never really gotten a good look at her face. He must be going stir crazy, he decided. He was getting a little too fixated on her. *Get a grip, Martin,* he scolded himself.

# CHAPTER 15

Audrey had a dilemma. Should she risk traveling to her old stomping grounds or wait until the restrictions of Level 4 were over? If she was stopped by police, she had no proof of residency. Her previous address in Hihi was where she had committed her last offence was when she was known as Audrey Wetherby. This new May Audrey Simmons had no known address. In fact, apart from her forged passport, she didn't even have a driver's license in her name. She was waiting for her new IDs to be sent to her. They were due to arrive in the mail within the next week or so. She had applied online for a new bank account and the debit card was also arriving in the mail. She decided she had better wait until she was prepared.

She had to admit she was attracted to her neighbor. It had been a while since she had indulged in any form of romantic passion. Audrey was bisexual, which opened up twice the playing field. This man was obviously available and lived alone—two of Audrey's essential criteria for a short-term arrangement. She picked up the phone and dialed his number. There was no answer. She left a short message.

"Martin, it's your neighbor, May. Just wanted to say thank you for the gloves. Appreciate the thought."

SHE TOOK A CUP OF COFFEE AND HER PHONE OUTSIDE, knowing she could sunbathe in the backyard without being disturbed this time by Mr. Street; with any luck, he had already finished off his last bottle of bourbon. But her peace was short-lived as she heard sirens approaching. They were heading up the hill behind her. *Fuck! They've found the body. That was quick!* She'd thought the old man would be dead for days, even weeks, before anyone found him. Her phone rang. She answered.

"May, it's Martin. Thanks for your call." He was shouting over the sound of the sirens. "Can you hear me? Or should I call you back?"

"Yes, call me back," she said.

"Okay, will do."

She was not in the mood for flirting with the neighbor. The discovery of the old man's body was unexpected. She needed to keep low for the next couple of days. She had also seen herself on the news as one of the passengers they were looking for. It was a surveillance video of her walking through security. She was glad she no longer owned the same outfit. Even so, she was too exposed. At least they had not found Mr. and Mrs. Simmons. She turned off her phone and went inside.

Audrey poured herself a glass of champagne. It calmed her and always gave her a sense of wellbeing. Her thoughts went to the day she had arrived in Auckland. She had been on a mission. When she decided to move into the cottage in Totara North, she knew she would have to dispose of the owners. Audrey was financially solvent thanks to past endeavors, but most of her funds were not available—at least, not yet.

The couple had been surprised when she called them for a meeting. She explained she had seen the cottage online and would like to make an offer but didn't want to go through the real estate agent. She said she was aware they would still have to pay the agent commission and she would cover that amount in the purchase. They seemed a little concerned with the arrangement but agreed to meet with her.

Audrey wore a blonde wig and extra padding to disguise her now slender physique. She had parked her car a distance from their house, walked to the front door, and rang the bell. They were a couple in their sixties or older. They invited her in and offered her a cup of tea or coffee. Audrey accepted gratefully as she opened her bag and pulled out a file and laid it on the table. When Mary Sutton returned with cucumber sandwiches, a fresh pot of tea, a small jug of milk, and a bowl of sugar, Audrey knew she would be able to take care of the situation much easier than she first thought. A simple distraction would enable her to pour the ingredients of a small vial into the milk jug and the meeting could begin.

Bruce and Mary talked about the economic situation now that the world was being hit with the global pandemic. "Awful, simply awful," they kept saying. "It is caused by all those terrible Chinese people. They started it."

Audrey nodded and listened patiently as Mary poured milk into her and her husband's teacups. "Milk? "she asked Audrey.

"No, thank you," she replied.

They sat and ate cucumber sandwiches and sipped their tea and discussed the cottage in Totara North. Audrey offered the asking price. They, of course, accepted. She said it would be a cash offer and asked for their bank account information so she could deposit the money. The couple suggested they should talk to their lawyer before signing any paperwork. Audrey agreed. She produced a sale and purchase agreement with all the details already filled in. "I just need your signature," she said. "Of course, you can get your lawyer to look at it first," she offered.

Bruce and Mary looked at the agreement. "It looks good enough to me," Bruce said. "I don't think we need to get his approval." Audrey passed him a pen. He signed the document and handed it to his wife to sign. "There," he said. "It's all yours."

"Your tea is getting cold. Want a top-up?" Mary asked as she made her and Bruce another cup.

"That would be lovely," Audrey said, putting the documents away in her file. She left a copy on the table for the nice couple.

Knowing the GHB would take effect within five to ten minutes, Audrey didn't have too long. "I don't suppose you could show me your garden," she suggested. "I noticed you have a beautiful collection of bromeliads."

"Of course," Mary said. "Let me give you some for the cottage."

Before leaving the table, Audrey picked up their copy of the agreement and returned it to her file. Not a good idea to leave evidence behind. She had been careful to wear gloves, saying she didn't want to risk getting the virus, and she hoped they understood.

They all walked out into the sunshine. Ten minutes later Audrey left the couple waving at the front door. She knew the poison would take effect any moment. She turned to see they had closed the door. *Good*, she thought. She didn't want them passing out on front doorstep. That would not be good.

The next day she had called on the couple again, this time to take them for a scenic drive out of the neighborhood in their old Holden. It was a long walk back to her car, but Audrey enjoyed the exercise on the warm autumn day.

The sirens had stopped. The phone rang. It was Martin.

# CHAPTER 16

Constable Patterson was quite surprised to find old Luke Street dead in his chair with a bottle of bourbon and an empty glass by his side. Knowing Luke lived alone, Patterson had decided to pop by to check on him.

He wondered if the old man had died of the virus. He took some photos of the scene and waited for the coroner to declare him dead. He noticed two small drops of blood on the floor. They looked quite fresh. He took a photo to be thorough but figured the old man had simply died of booze and old age. He asked them to take a sample of the blood anyway. The medics, like the coroner, were in full protective clothing. Zipping up old Luke in a bag, they loaded him into the back of the ambulance. The house was a mess. Dishes piled high on the bench, empty booze bottles cluttering the floor and kitchen table. Patterson knew he had a son living somewhere in Christchurch. One family member could attend. He would track him down and give him the news.

Patterson was concerned he had visited the woman in the cottage. Old Luke had sold off the cottage many years ago and yet he still acted as though he owned it. When he had a few drinks, he would wander down and harass the tenants who used to live there. Patterson decided he would make a visit to the woman to advise her of her neighbor's death and see how she was coping during the lockdown.

He had always liked the little heritage cottage. As he drove up the driveway, he saw a car parked in the carport. The government had insisted all residents stay home and only go out for essentials. He walked up the pathway that led to the back door and knocked. There was no reply. He knocked again. Still no reply. He looked in the window of the kitchen and saw a laptop sitting on the table. He left his card tucked in the edge of the door and headed back to his car. She must be out walking, he thought.

Driving down the driveway he stopped to talk to the neighbor in his garden. "Have you seen the lady from the cottage?" Patterson asked.

"She was there just a moment ago. I was talking to her on the phone," Martin replied.

"Well, she's not there now."

"Was there an accident up the hill?" Martin asked.

"Old man Luke died."

"Oh, that's a shame. He must have been in his eighties," Martin said.

"When was the last time you saw him?" Patterson asked.

"Oh, weeks ago. Saw him in the local pub."

Okay. You don't know if the lady in the cottage has seen him?"

"I wouldn't think so. May keeps pretty much to herself."

"You've met her, then?"

"Well, not officially. We have talked on the phone," Martin clarified.

"What did you say her name is?" Patterson asked.

"May something. I don't know her last name."

"I thought the cottage was for sale. Did she buy it?"

"I presume so. The sign's gone," Martin said.

""Okay. Gotta go. Thanks," Patterson said, turning to leave.

In his rearview mirror, Patterson noticed Martin watching as the police car disappeared down the drive, a confused look on his face.

Patterson had an uneasy feeling in the pit of his stomach. He was a good cop. His interest was in forensics, and he'd taken every course he could in the area. His gut told him to look into the old man's death and not just presume he died of natural causes. Maybe it was Covid-19.

# CHAPTER 17

Tracy and Keke heard the sirens and couldn't resist heading out the front door to see where the emergency crews were heading. With the fear of Covid-19 infecting everyone, they worried someone had called 111 with the symptoms. They watched the vehicles with lights flashing pass their corner and head toward the jetty.

"Call Steve and see if he knows what it is," Keke suggested.

"I don't want to disturb him," Tracy said.

"Oh, go on," Keke said, loving the excitement.

"How about we take a walk and see where they have gone?" Tracy suggested.

"Great idea."

The women grabbed their phones and headed down the street. Keke lived just past the Totara pub and it was about a mile away from the jetty. There was only one main street in the small town with a couple of hundred residents and a local school. The once thriving timber mill was now derelict. A local museum was only open upon request. It was a quiet community, with the local pub being its center and fishing being its staple recreation.

By the time the women reached the end of the road, the sirens had stopped but they could see the flashing lights atop the hill.

"That's old Luke's place," Keke said. "He must have taken ill. Or died."

"Nice little cottage," Tracy said, spying the cottage on the hill below all the activity.

"Yes. It's on the market. I know the real estate agent who is selling it—Rose Bright. She's a friend of mine."

"Do you think we can look at it?" Tracy asked. "My mother is looking for a cottage like that. It would be perfect for her."

"No problem. The place is empty, and Rose would have left a key hidden somewhere. I'll give her a call."

Rose picked up immediately. "Keke, how are you? How are you getting on in your bubble?"

"I have my friend Tracy staying with me. How are you? How are the kids?"

"Challenging to say the least. But we are all coping."

"That's good to hear. I'm calling because Tracy would like to look at the cottage you have listed by the jetty. She thinks her mother may like it. Is there a key somewhere? Would you mind if we take a look?"

"I am sure the owners won't mind," Rose said. "The key is under the flowerpot by the back door. You can't miss it. Actually, it would be good if you can keep an eye on the cottage during lockdown. We're not allowed to work during Level 4 except online. Hope the 'For Sale' sign is still standing upright."

"What 'For Sale' sign?" asked Keke. "There's no sign here."

"That's odd. Can't imagine why it has been removed. Hopefully the cottage is okay. The power is still on. Call me after you have walked through."

"Will do. Thanks, Rose," Keke said, then hung up.

As the women crossed the road, a police car was heading down the driveway. It stopped and the officer rolled down the window.

"What are you two doing out and about?" the officer asked.

"Just taking a quick walk," said Keke.

"Tracy, isn't it? Constable Patterson," the officer said. "How is Steve? What are you doing out here in this neck of the woods?"

"I'm staying with Keke during lockdown. Steve thought it would be safer for me," she replied.

"What happened up the hill?" Keke asked.

"Old man Luke has passed away," said Patterson.

"I thought so."

"You should not be straying too far from home," Pattern reminded them sternly.

"We were just heading back," Tracy said.

"Stay home and keep safe," Patterson called back as he drove toward the main highway.

"We should come back later," Tracy suggested, feeling a little guilty.

"Yep. Tomorrow. We will come back tomorrow morning."

# CHAPTER 18

udrey looked at the time. It was nine o'clock. This
morning she would take a drive to Mangonui and do
some food shopping, pick up more wine, and check
out her old neighborhood. Thank goodness for the virus. Every-
body would be wearing face masks. Even though she looked
considerably different from three years ago, she would feel a lot
less exposed wearing a mask.

She only passed one car on the fifteen-minute drive. Turning
right off the motorway she took the loop road onto the
Mangonui main street. She passed the little boutique which had
stocked her wardrobe for years, the book and lotto store, the pub,
and the waterfront restaurants. all closed and deserted. When she
reached the small dairy there was a small line outside—not like
the city supermarkets, where you had to queue for almost an
hour to be allowed inside. Social distancing was strict and
adhered to. Inside, there was tape on the floor, so customers
knew where they were expected to wait at the check-out.

Audrey was shocked to see a familiar face at the counter.
Three years on and the staff were just the same. She almost forgot

she looked different on the outside when she felt exactly the same on the inside. Audrey was surrounded by everything familiar and yet everything was completely different. She knew where to find every product on every shelf and yet the unfamiliar communal fear of catching the virus was evident. The few select shoppers were keeping the required distance. Due to the fear of catching Covid-19 from shopping carts, they were carrying multiple fabric bags bulging with product they would take home and wash in soapy water or spray with antibacterial spray.

She carried her supplies to the counter along with her shopping bags. She wore white disposable gloves and a face mask she had made out of a scarf and hair ties. She had seen how to do this on a Facebook post. She hid her green eyes behind sunglasses, knowing the check-out woman would be too preoccupied to make conversation. The lockdown was affecting everyone. The once close-knit community seemed scared and distant. Residents just wanted to return to the safety of their homes. She watched a man bend down to pick up a newspaper by the door only to repel backward when he realized it could be contaminated. It was a strange new world.

Then she saw him. He had parked his car next to hers. He hadn't changed one iota. She could feel her heart stop. She couldn't move. He looked right at her as he joined the line outside the store. *Fuck!* she thought. Her hands were shaking as she placed her shopping bags on the back seat and removed her gloves, placing them in a plastic bag. Climbing into the driver's seat, she sprayed her hands and her credit card with antibacterial spray while watching the man she had known so well. He was looking at his phone. She wondered why he was not wearing a mask. The line began to move. It was almost as though he knew what she was thinking and reached into his pocket, removing a mask and gloves in preparation for his turn to enter the store.

As Audrey started the car, he looked at her. She felt exposed, as though he knew it was her. But he couldn't. She began to back out, nearly hitting a car on the narrow road. She felt completely discombobulated. He had always had this effect on her.

When Audrey reached the main road, she headed south toward home.

# CHAPTER 19

R ose Bright had been in real estate for just over a year. It had proven to be a lucrative business until Covid-19 hit the country. Now real estate was not considered to be an essential business, which made her life difficult. She had settlements that could not take place until after the government reduced the alert system to Level 2 measures or below. Moving trucks were not considered to be essential businesses so she had clients who had sold their properties but could not move out or move in. Valuations could not take place; builders' reports could not be carried out. It was difficult. But Rose was diligent in her work and kept in touch with her clients, giving them updates and weekly stats. Buyers were still browsing the web, but viewings were not permitted.

When she had a call from Keke she was pleased to know someone could keep an eye on the little cottage she had on the market in Totara North. It was quite secluded, and the owners lived in Auckland. They had recently asked the tenants to vacate, leaving the little cottage vacant over the lockdown. She was concerned someone had taken down the "For Sale" sign. Maybe it had blown over in the wind and a neighbor had simply removed it.

She had emailed the owners a couple of times over the past two weeks but had not received a reply. She figured they were preoccupied with the lockdown. Rose lived in Coopers Beach and it was only a twenty-minute drive to Totara North. She wished she could carry out a general check of her properties, but with the Level 4 lockdown it simply wasn't permitted.

She would wait until she heard from Keke. She thought she might be breaking the rules by allowing a friend to view the cottage during lockdown. But in the end, she decided the owners would be happy to know someone was keeping an eye on their property.

# CHAPTER 20

"I t is beautiful!" Tracy walked from room to room. "You can see the view of the boats and the water from almost every room. Mum will simply love this place!"

"The kitchen is adorable. It feels as though you have stepped back in time to the early nineteen-hundreds," said Keke.

"How much do they want for it?" Tracy walked into the bedroom. "I can't believe they are selling it furnished." She opened up the wardrobe door. "Did you know there are clothes in the closet?" she asked Keke. "Why would there be clothes in the closet? Surely the tenants removed their personal belongings."

The women walked into the lounge and noticed a computer sitting on the small coffee table. They checked out the kitchen and saw there was fresh milk in the fridge, along with eggs, ham, and bottles of sauces. Wine bottles were placed in the door of the fridge.

"Someone is living here," Keke said.

"Shit! I thought you said it was vacant," Tracy replied.

"Rose said it was. We'd better get out of here."

The women quickly locked the back door and replaced the key under the flowerpot. As they headed down the driveway, they passed the guy they had seen at the jetty many times taking a walk.

"Morning," they said.

"Morning," he replied.

When Keke called Rose there was no reply. She left a message for her to call her back.

"I wonder who is living there?" Tracy said. "I wonder if they removed the 'For Sale' sign. Do you think it has been sold?" She thought a moment. "Or maybe the owners have a friend staying there during lockdown."

"Oh, of course. That would explain it. I wonder why Rose doesn't know," Keke said.

"I guess we will find out," Tracy said. "I have to say I felt like an intruder. It was really weird, eh?"

They giggled.

# CHAPTER 21

Martin wondered why the two women were walking down the driveway. It only led to his house and May's house. Maybe they were friends of hers. But residents were not supposed to go outside their immediate bubble. He noticed May's car was not in her carport. She must have gone shopping. He needed to go again soon too. They had told everyone not to binge-shop, but at the same time, it meant repeat visits to the store were required during the four-week lockdown.

He had just closed the front door when he heard her car. She was driving too fast up the driveway and into her carport. *She's in a bloody hurry. What is her problem?* Martin thought. He was feeling a bit pissed off. He had hoped they could get together, but she obviously wanted to be left alone. He watched out his window as she unloaded the groceries and carried them up the path and out of sight. The cottage was not visible from his house.

Yesterday he had made some phone calls around the neighborhood to discuss the passing of old Luke. Because of lockdown there would be no public funeral. Sad, really. The old man had been part of the community for a long time. He liked to take his old boat out and fish for hours. Martin knew old Luke had a son. He guessed that, after lockdown, the son would come north and handle things. Clean out the house, sell the boat.

Martin's phone beeped with a message. It was from his old friend, Jimmy Bromley. Jimmy had left three years ago for California with his new wife, Poppy. The message said he was back in town. Martin knew he had left under a dark cloud. His job and previous marriage had both collapsed. He had been a good cop, even promoted to detective constable before everything got fucked up. He had been working on the Audrey Wetherby case. Just when they'd thought they had her she had disappeared. No one had heard of her since. Jimmy had felt responsible. He'd led the case and he felt his reputation was tarnished.

Martin called him straightaway. Such a shame they couldn't meet. Jimmy and Poppy were back and staying in Mangonui with friends. Martin promised to catch up with them both when lockdown was over. He was pleased they were back. Jimmy said he'd been called back to assist with the Covid-19 situation. He was working on tracking down passengers from overseas flights that may have been contaminated with the virus.

# CHAPTER 22

F*uck! Fuck! Fuck!* Audrey had never expected to see him again. She had read he and Poppy had left for California. Now he was back and in Mangonui. He had been tracking her for years. Poppy had written her best-selling bloody book about Audrey's alleged murders. Alleged because they were never proven. Oh yes, they had her DNA at various locations. But she had never killed Poppy's brother. That was the one murder she never actually did and was the one murder that nearly got her caught. Poppy had been tenacious in tracking her down. Audrey suspected she was back, too.

Thank goodness for lockdown. Trouble was, it was more difficult to be seen out and about. Cops were beginning to do random roadblocks to check if residents were staying close to their neighborhoods for shopping. Audrey had only two choices to shop: Kaeo or Mangonui. Both were the same distance apart and both had police looking for her as a missing passenger of AIRNZ1. Both had her DNA on record, and now with Bromley in town, she would have to watch her back. At least she had enough supplies to last her a couple of weeks. In the meantime, she would keep close to home.

She opened her wardrobe to change her clothes and noticed her black hat was on the ground. She distinctly remembered putting it on the top shelf before she went out. Someone had been inside, she realized. Someone had been snooping around the cottage. Who? Was it Martin? Unlikely. He didn't seem the sort of guy to break and enter. It wouldn't be the police. They would need a search warrant. Who?

She dialed Martin's number. "I don't suppose you saw anyone at my cottage when I was gone, did you?" she asked sweetly.

"I did see a couple of women walking down the driveway. I've seen them before. They often hang out at the jetty. I don't know their names. I can find out for you," he offered.

"Thanks. That would be great." She hung up.

*Fuck! Two women. Who are they?* She tried to rationalize their presence. Maybe they were real estate agents checking on the cottage. *Damn! I thought they were not allowed to be working.* Martin had said they lived locally. She knew he would find out their names. He would use it as an excuse to call her back.

She was right. He would call back.

# CHAPTER 23

Keke was in seventh heaven. She loved a good mystery. Rose said no one was supposed to be staying in the cottage. The owners had made it quite clear they wanted it vacant for buyer viewings. Maybe the owners had changed their mind when the country went into lockdown. Maybe they had a friend staying there. Rose asked Keke to check on who it was. Keke was only too pleased to help. Who was the stranger living in the cottage?

Tracy had laughed at her enthusiasm. "It's most likely just a relative of the owners," she said.

Keke thought it strange the owners had not notified Rose. "It's too late to go over today," she said. "Will you come with me tomorrow?"

"Of course," said Tracy. "I wouldn't let you go alone. Anyway, I would like to see who owns all those designer clothes. Did you see the hats? Super classy, whoever she is."

When Detective Constable Mason called his wife that evening, he got an earful about the secret woman living in the cottage by the jetty.

"You shouldn't be meeting other people during lockdown," he complained. "You know the rules—keep in your own bubble."

"We will keep our distance," she said. "We are just going to knock at the door and say we are neighborhood watch and checking on the property as we understood it was vacant and on the market."

"She doesn't have to tell you anything," he said. "Just be careful."

"Don't worry," said Tracy. "If we think there's something weird going on, we will let you know."

"It is Keke's idea, isn't it?" Mason said. "She is getting you into this."

"You know how much she enjoys a good mystery." Tracy laughed. "Love you."

"Love you," Mason replied.

"What did Steve say?" Keke asked when Tracy joined her in the lounge.

"He said we shouldn't be doing this in lockdown."

"I know. We are naughty." Keke giggled.

As they watched the evening news, there was a report about how one of the passengers from the Air New Zealand flight had still not been located. She had been seated within two meters of a known case. They showed video footage of the woman leaving the airport. "If anyone has seen this woman, please contact your nearest police station."

"I wonder why she has not come forward," Keke said.

"She's most likely already in self-isolation," replied Tracy. "Obviously doesn't want the media exposure. Can't say I blame her."

# CHAPTER 24

Jimmy and Poppy were glad to be back. It wasn't an easy decision. Poppy knew Jimmy had reservations about going back to working in law enforcement. This time he was going to be working as a private detective with the Covid-19 contact tracing division. The division had already tracked over four thousand cases before the end of the first week of lockdown.

He'd told her that for the most part it was a fairly easy process. Some were more difficult. He was still trying to track down a woman who had been sitting two seats away from an infected case on an Air New Zealand flight from Los Angeles ten days ago. Her name was Anna Ward. Nice-looking, dark long hair, slender features, in her forties, he guessed.

They were staying with friends of Poppy during the lockdown period. Then they would look at buying a place. Poppy had her eye on a cute heritage cottage in Totara North, built around 1910. She had seen it on Trademe and had enquired with the agent. Unfortunately, all real estate was put on hold until the government lowered the level status, and this would take quite a few weeks yet. The agent had sent her a packet of information.

She was tempted to take a drive past and look at it, but it seemed as though you couldn't see well from the street.

If Jimmy had any job out that way, she could beg him to take her. There were not many properties on the market in rural northland. Not like in the big cities, and during lockdown there were even fewer to choose from.

She looked over at Jimmy on his computer. This afternoon he had tracked the missing woman's movement to a cab company. They found the cabbie and he said he had taken her to a secondhand car place. Jimmy was talking to the guy on the phone. "A white Nissan, registration CTP133. Got it. Thanks."

# Chapter 25

Audrey had a sixth sense something was not right. She couldn't put her finger on it, but her instincts were usually spot-on. She knew she was being tracked by the Covid-19 tracing division. She never used a smartphone. Her burner phone was always turned off and she was diligent at replacing the sims cards regularly. She was a pro at not being located when she didn't want to be. She had considered filling out the form online advising them she had been on the plane but showing no symptoms and was in self-isolation since leaving the airport. But chances were they would want to test her and that was not going to happen. When she was in Auckland, she changed the registration plate on her car using black and white paint. Now it read OIB188. She also put a black stripe using black tape along each side of the vehicle. She knew eventually they would be looking for her car. Now, both the name Anna Ward and the car did not exist.

When she heard footsteps and voices coming up her path, she had two choices: to hide or answer the door. She saw two women coming up the back steps toward the kitchen door. She presumed these were the two women who had gone through her stuff. They obviously knew where the key was. She would pretend virus fear and talk to them through the door. Putting on her sunglasses, she grabbed a scarf and wrapped it around her face.

There they were. Stupid smiling faces staring at her through the glass.

"Sorry, I am isolating and don't want to come outside," she called out.

"Oh, we are too," the chubby one said. "My name is Keke. I'm a neighbor. This is my friend Tracy. She is staying with me. We understood the house is on the market and my friend is interested in buying it. Are you the owner?"

Audrey could tell they were on a fact-finding mission. No one would be going house-hunting during lockdown. Someone had clearly put them up to this. She had to think fast.

"I'm sorry, did you say you were interested in buying the cottage?" she said, stalling for time.

"Yes, my friend is."

"I'm sorry, but this is not a good time. The house is not on the market. It has been taken off during lockdown. I don't suppose you noticed the sign has been removed."

"Yes, we did notice. But my friend is the real estate agent and she said it was still for sale."

There it was. They were snooping on behalf of the real estate agent. "She's wrong. I'm looking after the property. If you want to leave your address and phone number, I can pass it on to the owners and they can follow up with you when all this is over."

"That would be great," Keke said.

Audrey left Keke looking in her handbag and returned to her bedroom to change. She needed some fresh air. On her way out she picked up the woman's business card. She would deal with her later. Maybe what she needed was a distraction . . . and perhaps her sexy neighbor could just provide that.

# CHAPTER 26

Martin noticed the two women did not stay long at the cottage. He guessed May had not let them in. He didn't blame her. Lockdown was not a time to go visiting. He wondered what they wanted. Shortly after they left, he saw May coming down the path and heading toward his house. *Shit!* He panicked. He had about thirty seconds to make himself look desirable. By the time she was knocking at the door, he knew thirty seconds wasn't going to do it.

She looked beautiful. "I don't suppose the offer to share your bubble is still open?" she asked.

"Absolutely! Come on in."

She smelled like apple blossom. "I'm glad you're here. I was beginning to go stir crazy here by myself."

"I know what you mean," Martin replied.

They sat at the table and chatted. She was easy to talk to and before long he had shared the past twenty years of his life. She was not as forthcoming. After a bottle of wine and an hour of conversation Martin realized he still knew very little about the beautiful woman sitting in front of him. When his phone buzzed on the table, she insisted he answer it.

It was Jimmy and Poppy. Poppy wanted to know if he knew anything about the little cottage on the market.

"Yes, funny you should ask. I have someone here who can give you all the details." He put the phone on speaker.

"May, meet Jimmy and Poppy, good friends of mine. They have just returned from the States. Poppy is interested in your little cottage."

"Oh. Hi May," Poppy said. "You own the cottage? Is it still on the market?"

"Ah, no. Sorry." Audrey paused. "The owners have taken it off the market. At least until lockdown is over."

"Oh, that is great! It means we can look at it after lockdown. You are living there? Isn't it simply wonderful? I just love old cottages . . . and the view! How long are you staying there?"

"Just for a few weeks. The owners are friends of mine."

"So, Martin, you guys know each other?" Jimmy asked.

"Just as neighbors," Martin explained. "We are single bubbles that are co-mingling."

Jimmy laughed.

"Well, stay safe. Nice to meet you, May. Watch out for that guy," Poppy warned.

"Bye."

"Bye."

Martin apologized for putting her on the spot. "Sorry about that."

Audrey knew she had dodged a bullet. She was sure the people on the phone had been Jimmy and Poppy Bromley. Fate seemed to be putting her in their path and it was dangerous. What was the chance her neighbor would know the two people that could put her away for the rest of her life? This was not good. They would have no idea she was back in New Zealand, and her new accent, disguising any remnant of her original voice, was a sure safeguard, but it was dangerous being so close to their good friend. "I have to head back," she said. "I have a lot of work to catch up on. Thanks for the drinks."

"Would you like to come for dinner tomorrow night?"

"I will let you know tomorrow. Is that okay?" she said.

He walked her to the door. She seemed distracted and on edge. He wanted to touch her in some way. He raised his hand to brush away a stray hair that had escaped onto her forehead. She recoiled, as if he was being too familiar. It was a mistake. But she was his future. He was sure about that.

# CHAPTER 27

Keke was beside herself. "Did you see her? It looked as though she was in disguise. All covered up. What was that all about? A bit overboard, don't you think? She is hiding something. I just know it."

Tracy had been listening to Keke's stream of incessant chatter for the past half hour. "Why don't you talk to Rose? She can talk to the owners."

"Good idea. I will."

Tracy could hear Keke in the next room giving Rose the full rundown on their meeting with the strange woman in the cottage. "She was all covered up and wouldn't let us in," she heard Keke say.

"So?" Tracy asked when Keke had finally finished the call. "Is she going to call the owners?"

"Yes. She said she will call them and call me straight back. She thought it strange the woman asked for my address and phone number. She has a point there. Why did she ask for my address? Especially when I said the real estate agent is my friend. You don't suppose I have to worry, do you?"

"What do you think she would do to you?" Tracy laughed. "Hit you with her scarf? Get real, Keke. She's just like a lot of people—stressed out with all the Covid-19 news."

That night Tracy had her nightly catch-up with her husband and filled him in on the day's adventure. Mason thought the woman's reaction was justified based on Tracy and Keke's actions. "She's in lockdown, like all of us. She would not have felt comfortable with two strangers knocking at her door asking her questions."

Tracy agreed but admitted it was a bit of fun. "Now we're waiting for Rose, the real estate agent, to check with the owners. They never told her they had taken the property off the market."

Rose called back later that evening. She had tried many times to contact the owners. "They are not returning my calls," she explained. "I have to say it is all rather strange. They're usually really prompt at replying to my emails. If I haven't heard back from them by tomorrow afternoon, I will try and track down a relative." She asked Keke to contact her if the woman got in touch with her. "Get her name and phone number so I can call her if you can."

Keke had an idea, and she pitched it to Tracy. "If we get the registration number of her car, Steve could find out who she is. Do you think he would do that?"

"Now you're going too far, Keke. She's just a nice lady looking after the cottage for her friends. Let's see what Rose says tomorrow," Tracy said.

Keke frowned. "I wish I hadn't given her my address and phone number."

# CHAPTER 28

F*uck! Fuck! Fuck!* Audrey was pacing up and down the kitchen with a glass of wine in hand. *How the hell did this happen? How was I to know the bloody neighbor was friends with Jimmy and Poppy Bromley?*

She cursed inwardly. She'd read they had left for the States after she had disappeared. What an awful coincidence that they'd returned the same time as her. It was the Covid-19 scare. Closing the New Zealand borders caused many Kiwis to return while they could. The USA was dealing with much higher rates of infection. It was safer here.

Poppy wanted to buy the cottage. Thank God no one could view properties during the lockdown. There were so few properties on the market and the cottage was such a gem, no wonder she wanted to buy it. And those bloody neighbors poking their noses around. She was sure they would report back to the agent. At least no one could contact the owners. She had made sure of that.

Living in rural New Zealand was a gossiper's dream location. Especially in the tiny village of Totara North. The small coastal villages dotting the coastline in the far north—Mangonui,

Coopers Beach, Cable Bay, Taipa—each had their own gossip pool and collectively were forced to share the small selection of shops and restaurants. The days of shopping and dining out were over. The local Mangonui dairy did offer a pack-and-collect service but there were no home deliveries. It meant all locals had to do their weekly shopping in the same small group of shops. With no shop in Totara North, it forced all residents to venture out of the village and mingle with neighboring towns.

She looked at the short note left by the neighbors. Keke's address was less than a mile up the road toward the main highway. She opened her computer and did a search. She was unmarried and ran a small bed-and-breakfast operation, which meant it would be closed during the lockdown. She was with a friend. Audrey wondered if the friend was staying with her. Most likely she was, as they would have to be in same bubble to be out in public together.

She had a decision to make. She couldn't risk spending any more time with Martin. As tempting as it was, he was danger. She called him.

"Martin, May here. I am so sorry, but I feel like just keeping in my little bubble for a while. Can I take a rain check on dinner? Great. Thanks. Catch up later."

She could tell he was disappointed.

# CHAPTER 29

Constable Patterson received the result from the Covid-19 test on old Luke. It was negative. The coroner has advised his death was caused by natural causes. Case closed. He never heard back from the woman in the cottage but with old Luke being no risk, there was no need to follow up.

The lockdown was causing problems throughout the Kaeo area. Burglaries were up and the local youths were not adhering to the lockdown rules. Residents were not keeping to their immediate neighborhood, taking shopping trips to Kerikeri, thirty minutes away, rather than shopping locally. There was a large farming community in the area and farmers were still operating as normal, and local stock supplies retailers were operating during lockdown on limited hours. Unfortunately, vegetable crops were being left to rot in the ground. Unless the suppliers were registered suppliers to supermarkets, they could not sell and distribute their merchandise. It was difficult times for many New Zealanders.

. . .

He checked his emails and recognized a small white Nissan wanted by the Covid-19 tracing team. It looked very much like the white Nissan he had seen parked at the cottage. He would take a drive up to Totara North today and check it out, and do a drive down to the jetty to make sure residents were adhering to the "no boating" rules.

He checked his messages. There was a voicemail from Rose Bright, a real estate agent, requesting he call her.

Patterson knew Rose. They had met on a number of occasions. He called her immediately.

"Rose, Constable Patterson here. You called me?"

"You are being very formal, Andy," she teased. "Yes. I have a situation and was hoping you could help."

"Of course. What is it?" He could tell by the tone of her voice that something was wrong.

"There is a property in Totara North I have listed, and the owners informed me a few weeks ago the tenants had vacated the property. However, my friend who lives in Totara North says there is a woman living in the house. The woman said she was a friend of the owners, but my friend thought she was acting strangely. I have not been able to contact the owners for a couple of weeks. I'm worried. They always return my calls. My 'For Sale' sign has been removed and I cannot carry out any real estate work while we are in lockdown."

"Where do the owners live?"

"They live in Auckland. Remuera. I have their address."

"What would you like me to do?" Patterson asked.

"Could you check on the house? It's a little cottage down by the jetty."

"Up on the hill, below old man Luke's property?" Patterson was now a lot more interested.

"Yes, that is the one. I was sorry to hear about Luke Street.

He was a longtime resident of Totara North. They will miss him; he was a regular down at the old pub."

"I was planning on heading out there later on this afternoon. I'll check on your mystery woman then and let you know."

"I owe you," Rose said. "Why don't you come around afterwards. I am going a little crazy being locked in. I have a leg of lamb we could share for dinner. Are you still a bubble of one?" she asked.

Patterson laughed. He had always fancied Rose Bright. "Yes, are you?"

"You know me. All work and no play. No time for relationships."

"Then I will come by about six. I will be off-duty then."

"Great, see you then."

Patterson's mood definitely picked up. Rose Bright. She was some sexy woman. He would be only too happy to help her out.

# CHAPTER 30

It was late in the afternoon when Audrey decided to take a walk down to the jetty. She had a favorite spot on the deck of the old store. She realized it was now someone's holiday home but was vacant during the lockdown. The historic old building was built over the water and provided a perfect place to sit unnoticed by the occasional neighbor strolling down the jetty or walking the nearby shore.

Today she was surprised to see a woman sitting on the deck gazing quietly out to sea. She wore a large red scarf wrapped around her head and across her face. The weather was getting a little cooler, with an autumn breeze blowing in from across the harbor. Audrey stood quietly observing her and was about to leave when the woman turned.

"Don't go," she said. "Join me."

Audrey, keeping the required distance, chose a bench farther down the deck. "I thought no one lived here," she said.

"No one does." The woman laughed. "I just come down here to get some fresh air."

"So do I," Audrey said.

"Would you like some champagne?" the woman asked as she reached into her bag and extracted two small bottles of Lindauer Brut.

"That would be perfect." She took the bottle from the woman, screwed open the top, and took a sip. "I'm May," she offered.

"Kathy Lane," the woman said. "Nice to meet you."

Champagne was not the only thing the women had in common. As they talked, Audrey learned Kathy had just returned from California too. She had come back to be with her father, who lived in an old heritage house near the pub. "He has not been well and when I heard New Zealand would be closing their borders, I took the next plane," Kathy explained.

"Do you like being back in New Zealand?" Audrey asked.

"I do and I don't. I miss the great restaurants, live music, Mexican food, and the theater, but I love the beauty of New Zealand. I have been gone so long I really don't have any friends here anymore," she confided.

Audrey liked this woman. "Well, we can be friends. I'm here alone and could do with some company."

"That would be wonderful," Kathy said.

As they finished their champagne the wind was beginning to turn colder.

"We must get back before we freeze to death," Kathy said. "Shall we meet here tomorrow, same time?" she asked.

"I will bring the champagne next time," Audrey offered.


It was day thirteen of lockdown. The government announced that it looked as though the strict measures were working, with numbers of infected cases beginning to decrease. It was too early to tell yet, they were saying, but they hoped to completely stop the virus in its tracks. Not just contain it, as other countries were trying to achieve, but New Zealand wanted to eradicate it completely. The numbers of daily infected cases had halved in the last few days. Two more weeks to go, and then the government would advise if the Level 4 lockdown could be reduced. Audrey knew she only had two more weeks of living in the cottage. Meeting Kathy might be her ticket to new accommodation. Tomorrow she would find out more about where they were living and do some checking into her family's background.

When Audrey arrived back at the cottage there was another card in the door from Constable Patterson. He had written on the back, "Call me, please." *Fuck! What does he want?* Rather than risk him returning to the cottage, she made the call.

"Constable Patterson, you asked me to call you. It's May Simmons."

"Oh, thank you, May, for returning my call. I just have a couple of questions for you. You may have heard—Luke Street, who lives above the cottage, has just died. I wanted you to know. He mentioned he met you a week ago." He waited for her response.

"Yes, I did meet him. Sorry to hear about him dying."

"He mentioned you have purchased the cottage off the Suttons?"

"He must have been mistaken. I am only just looking after the cottage for them while we are in lockdown. They were worried about it being vacant."

"I had a call from the real estate agent to say the sign had been removed and the owners had not mentioned you would be staying in the cottage."

"Oh, it was just last-minute. They're good friends of mine. They said they could not get up here to the cottage as they were going to be staying with friends in a small town outside Hamilton somewhere. An off-the-grid-type property during lockdown."

"Do you have their contact information in Queenstown?" Patterson asked.

"Sorry, I don't. I don't imagine they get cell coverage there," she offered.

"That would explain why they are not answering their phones or responding to emails. The real estate agent is trying to locate them."

"I'm sorry, I can't help you, constable."

"Please let me know if you hear from them," Patterson said.

"I will," Audrey agreed.

The conversation had gone well. Audrey figured she had at least a couple of weeks before more questions would be asked. In the meantime, she would enjoy living in the quaint seaside cottage and getting to know her new friend.

# CHAPTER 31

Keke was beside herself. All Rose could talk about was her evening with Constable Patterson.

"Oh, Keke, he is simply gorgeous. I wish he could have stayed all night, but he got called out at three o'clock with a madman shooting a rifle in Matang."

"What about the woman in the cottage?" Keke asked.

"Oh, he spoke to her. Apparently, the owners asked her to stay in the cottage during lockdown. They are staying with friends in a place with no cell coverage outside Hamilton somewhere. There is nothing I can do anyway until after lockdown," Rose said.

Keke was disappointed. She had really hoped the woman was trespassing, hiding out, or worse, a mass murderer. "I guess that is that, then."

After she hung up, Keke called out to Tracy, "I'm just taking a walk down to the jetty. Wanna come?"

"You go. I'm in the middle of great chapter. See you later," Tracy replied.

It was an excuse to do some more snooping. Keke didn't

want to believe the woman was who she said she was. Maybe there was mail in her letterbox. Totara North had rural mail delivered. Letterboxes were grouped together in a safe location for the mail van to pull over on the narrow street. The woman's mailbox was quite a way down the road from the cottage entrance. Keke could easily check her box with no one noticing. She had picked up a few promotional flyers so she could put them in the boxes if anyone caught her.

Opening the box, she saw a pile of letters. Two from banks, one from the Department of Motor Vehicles. The name on the envelopes was May A. Simmons. She took a quick photo of an envelope and quickly closed the box. *I know her name now,* Keke thought with excitement. She couldn't wait to get back and do some research. *There can't be too many May A. Simmonses in New Zealand.*

"What are you posting?"

Keke's heart was racing. She was caught. She watched as May opened the letterbox and removed her mail. The woman had a scarf wrapped around her face. Again, it was difficult to make out her features, but Keke could see she was an attractive woman. Forties, she guessed.

"Just some flyers," Keke said. "How are you enjoying your stay in the cottage?"

"It's peaceful," the woman replied as closed the letterbox. "But I enjoy the quietness."

Keke was careful to keep the required distance from her. "It's a shame you're here at such an awful time."

"Awful?" the woman asked.

"The lockdown," Keke explained.

"Oh, yes." The woman seemed preoccupied as she looked at the bundle of letters.

"Stay safe," Keke offered as she made her way back toward

her home. When she turned, the woman was opening some of the envelopes. Must be important mail, she thought. From the addresses on the envelopes, Keke guessed the woman could be getting new ID cards. Driver's license, credit cards. She didn't trust the woman. May could have made up the whole story about the owners. Keke noticed her middle initial was "A." Ann, Annabel, Audrey? Little did Keke know she had made a very serious mistake. No one snooped on Audrey and came out alive.

# CHAPTER 32

Kathy loved her family home. She was born in the old heritage house forty-one years ago. Her childhood and teenage years were spent fishing on her dad's boat and helping her mum in the garden. Kathy had kept her love of gardening. Now that she was home and her dad was alone, she was taking advantage of the lockdown to get the garden back to where it used to be before her mother passed away. It had been two years now and she could tell her dad was still lost without her. At eighty-two his health was suffering, and he had developed a very bad cough. She was hesitant to take him to the doctor with the Covid-19 virus known for attacking the elderly. She was the only child and came late in her parents' lives. She figured that was why she was so spoiled growing up. She knew the house would be hers one day. Then she would give up her job in California and move here permanently.

She was looking forward to meeting with May. It was almost four o'clock. She called out to her dad she was going to take a walk down to the jetty. "Be back soon," she said. She grabbed a warm jacket and her bag and climbed down the steep pathway to the road. Many old houses in Totara North were perched up on the Totara hills and accesses were often steep and quite precarious. She wondered how her dad coped, living alone here.

May was there waiting for her, such a beautiful woman. Kathy realized she didn't really know much about her. She had spent their last conversation talking about herself. How had that happened? She was usually a good listener. May waved as she walked onto the deck. She was already prepared with champagne and two glasses.

"I thought we could do it in style," Audrey said, passing her a full glass of bubbles.

"So," Kathy said, "tell me all about you. What has brought you here to our little village?"

"I'm here looking after my friends' cottage during lockdown. They couldn't get up here from Auckland, so I offered to stay a few weeks," May replied.

"What do you do when you're not house-sitting?" Kathy asked.

"I'm a researcher."

"You research what?" Kathy was interested.

"I research bees and their potential impact on native flora." May changed the subject. "Tell me about your dad. You mentioned he has lived here his whole life and you were born here. Do you ever think you will come back here to live?"

"My dad is eighty-two and not well. I'm worried about him. I came back to be with him during lockdown. I didn't want him here all by himself."

"You said you are a lawyer," May said. "What law do you specialize in?"

"I'm lucky," Kathy said. "I work in conveyancing. I have my own practice so can work from home."

The women opened the second small bottle of champagne

May had brought, and May produced a packet of potato crisps. "Sorry I didn't bring appetizers, but all the restaurants are closed," she joked. "And I hate to cook."

"Then you can share our bubble," Kathy offered. "It's not good be all alone during lockdown. I'm a great cook. Tonight, we're having steak and salad, my dad's favorite. Please join us."

May seemed pleased with the invite. "I would love to. What time?"

"Gosh, it's six already. How about seven? Is that OK?" Kathy asked.

"Perfect."

# CHAPTER 33

J immy Bromley was having no luck tracking the missing Anna Ward. He had asked for police to keep an eye out for the registration number. With their new scanning automatic number plate recognition cameras, police cars could scan number plates and alert police to any information that could be of interest to them. So far Anna Ward's white Nissan had not been located. She had not checked into a hotel or motel. He had contacted every Anna Ward living in New Zealand to avail. There were many, but not one had just returned from overseas prior to lockdown. He wondered if this woman did not want to be found. He saw she had traveled from LAX, but trying to track her in the USA would be extremely time-consuming and Anna Ward was a common name with over three hundred profiles on LinkedIn. He was sure of the number—he had looked at them all.

Bromley had put out a photo of a surveillance blurred image of Anna Ward along with a photo of the same white Nissan car and the registration number to the media. Maybe the public could help.

Bromley looked at the latest Covid-19 statistics for day fourteen of lockdown.

Total number of cases: 1,210
Total number of new cases: 50
Total number of recovered cases: 282
Total number of tests: 46,875
Total number of deaths: 1
Total number of cases in intensive care: 4 (1 critical)
Total number confirmed as community transference: 1%
Total number of infected clusters: 1%
Total number still to be analyzed: 14%

The ethnicity breakdown after two weeks at Level 4 was 73.3 percent European, 8.5 percent Asian, 7.8 percent Maori, and 3.4 percent Pacific Islanders. Forty-one percent of all infected cases had been traced to overseas contact. He presumed Anna Ward could easily add to this figure. He had checked the health line and all hospitals to see if she had been in contact with them. No one had heard from her.

He gave a call to his friend Martin. Poppy had been nagging him to take a trip to Totara North to look at the cottage from the outside. "Go on," she had said. "You can always say you are doing a follow-up to a lead."

"'Tell lies,' you mean," Jimmy had replied.

When he called Martin, he was surprised to hear he wasn't well.

"Been coughing all day," his friend said. "I have a temperature too."

"Sounds like you should get tested," Bromley suggested. "Have you been around anyone since lockdown? It has been two weeks now."

"Only the woman from the cottage. I haven't even been out to go shopping in two weeks."

"You don't sound good." Bromley was concerned. "Poppy wants me to have a look at the cottage and I was going to stop by. Don't think it's a good idea if you are feeling unwell, though. Seriously, man, you need to get tested."

"Yes. You're right. I can't imagine I have the virus, but it's a good idea to check."

"They are doing testing at Kaitaia Hospital and in Kerikeri," Bromley said. "It's too late now; they close at two o'clock. They open at nine o'clock."

"Thanks, Jimmy, I'll head off to Kaitaia tomorrow morning."

"Take care of yourself."

Jimmy told Poppy about Martin. She was concerned. "How could he catch it being in isolation for two weeks?" she asked.

"He said he had only seen the woman from the cottage. If he tests positive, she will need to be tested too."

"How awful!" Poppy said. "I really hope he's okay."

# CHAPTER 34

Keke and Tracy were settled down with their nightly glass of wine watching the six o'clock news when Keke let out a scream. "Holy cow! That looks like May's car! And it looks a little like her in the surveillance photo. Do you think she's the missing woman under a different name?"

The segment about the passenger from the Air New Zealand flight ended, and Keke turned to Tracy. "I didn't tell you because I knew you would think I'm crazy, but I checked out her mail today and found out her name is May A. Simmons. I'm going to sneak over there tonight and see what the number plate on her car says. I knew there was something strange about her."

"You are crazy." Tracy grinned. "You just want some excitement. Two weeks of being locked in is getting to you."

Keke smiled at her friend and shrugged. "I'm going over there anyway. It's dark about seven-thirty these days. Are you coming with me?"

Tracy refused. "No way. What if she sees you?"

"I'll be careful. You can't see the carport from the cottage. I'll have to dodge the guy next door to her. I'll just use my phone for light." Keke's eyes were lit up with excitement. She was simply ecstatic with the thought of hunting down the missing woman.

By seven-thirty Keke was dressed all in black with a black hoodie. She figured most residents would be watching TV or on their computers like the rest of the world during the pandemic. She doubted anyone would be looking out their window. New Zealanders had a specific telephone number to call to complain about anyone not adhering to the strict Level 4 rules. Thousands of calls had been made in the past two weeks and hundreds of cases had resulted in fines. She didn't want to be one of them.

The road was deserted. She passed the pub, the museum, and the old sawmill, and stood quietly in the shadows at the entrance to the cottage. The full moon was filtered by heavy cloud. The neighbor's curtains were closed. She turned the corner at the top of the driveway toward the cottage. *Shit! The car is gone! Damn!* Keke cursed. May had obviously gone out. But where? Keke had no choice but to return home.

# CHAPTER 35

Keke wasn't the only resident of Totara North who had recognized the white Nissan car. Martin had also recognized it. But upon checking the number plate, he realized the registration was different. He had looked as soon as he saw it on the news. Not long after, he heard May driving away. He wondered where she could be going. The shops were closed, and people were supposed to stay home.

His throat was hurting like hell. Jimmy was right—he would go to the hospital tomorrow morning and check he did not have Covid-19. Being over sixty, he was in the vulnerable age group. Most of New Zealand's cases were people aged in their twenties and thirties because that was the age group that returned home when they heard the borders were closing. Unfortunately, many brought the virus with them. He figured that was why the country's death rate was so low compared to the total number of cases.

He had been disappointed when May cancelled their dinner date. Now he was pleased because if he had the virus, he certainly didn't want to pass it on to her. He knew it could not have been her who had given it to him. It had only been a few days since they shared a bottle of wine. He looked up the time it takes to get infected; the information online said it could be anywhere from one to fourteen days. *Guess she could have given it to me,* he surmised. He also read it takes about a week to get very ill. Eighty percent of cases only experienced mild to moderate symptoms. He hoped he was one of those if it was confirmed he had it. He also knew he would have to wait a few days for the test results, although he'd heard that anyone who tested positive would be notified pretty quickly.

He knew to stay in bed. He was asleep when Audrey's car returned up the driveway.

# CHAPTER 36

The three of them sat around the dinner table enjoying good food, good wine, and good conversation. Audrey found Kathy and her father to be excellent company. She was particular about choosing who to spend her time with. An introvert by nature, Audrey usually preferred her own company to others. However, Kathy was different from most people she came in contact with. She was smart, funny, and beautiful. Audrey had fallen for a woman before, but it did not end well. Since then she had only slept with men. Her neighbor might have been her next choice if she had not met Kathy.

Kathy's father told stories of the early days in Totara North. When the sawmill was thriving, and the town was important to the development of the north. In 1870 Thomas Lane and William Brown had set up a boat-building enterprise called Lane and Brown, and were renowned for using only the best-quality kauri and hardwood timbers. They built ships up to 350 tons at Totara North and employed up to one hundred men. When the shipbuilding industry declined, the firm expanded its timber milling business. The timber mill known as Lane and Sons closed down in 2004. Today, all that remained of it was a crumbling old derelict building. Totara North was once home to the most successful kauri gum traders in the world, with hundreds of gum diggers. The old offices had been converted into The Gum Store, a bar and café on the main drag, Totara North Road.

It was late when Audrey said goodnight. Kathy walked her outside. "You drove here?" she said, spotting Audrey's little white car.

"I wasn't sure how far down the waterfront you lived and didn't want to get lost in the dark," she replied.

"Goodnight," Kathy said. "See you tomorrow for champagne on our deck?"

"Absolutely. Bye."

Audrey made the two-minute drive home with a happy heart. Kathy would make her life here a lot more palatable. In fact, she hoped meeting Kathy may even provide her with what she needed: a new place to stay. The cottage was causing too much attention. Too many nosy neighbors.

# CHAPTER 37

It was ten o'clock before Martin Melrose arrived at the testing tent outside Kaitaia Hospital. He was feeling a lot worse today and was pleased to get it over with and return home to bed. He hoped it was only the flu, but had a nagging feeling it was the dreaded virus.

He missed his daily walks to the jetty. He listened to the daily update on Covid-19 in New Zealand and was pleased to see new cases only totaled twenty-nine since yesterday. The lockdown was definitely working. The government announced, however, that Level 4 would stay in place for the full period of four weeks. So, two more weeks to go. He also heard that if he did test positive for the virus, he could register on his phone with the District Health Board and they could use new technology to trace any other phones he had been close to during the last few weeks when he contracted the virus. This technology was coming out of Singapore and the government had registered to obtain the technology for New Zealand.

His head and his throat hurt. He was getting worse. Martin had stopped for supplies on the way home, not that he felt like eating, but the packets of Panadol painkillers, throat lozenges and cough medicine, fresh lemons, and six bottles of water were a godsend.

He set up all his supplies on the bedside table along with his phone ringer switched to silent and prepared for a few days of complete rest.

He didn't hear the phone vibrating beside him as he fell into a troubled sleep.

# CHAPTER 38

Keke was determined to check May's car today. Tracy had already decided she didn't want to get involved with what she referred to as Keke's "crazy scheming" so Keke was alone on her walk to the cottage. It was early evening, about five-thirty, and the street was empty. She walked all the way to the jetty to find it abandoned. Did she dare to walk up the driveway to the cottage? She began to have second thoughts. Her encounter with May at her letterbox may have already created suspicion. But Keke couldn't resist as she came to the concrete driveway and made her way cautiously toward the carport. There was no sign of the man next door. She was grateful to see his curtains were closed.

Turning right, she walked up May's driveway, where she could clearly see May's white car in the carport. She didn't dare to go too close. She jotted down the registration number and noticed the car had a black stripe down the side. *Damn!* she thought. She didn't remember the car on the TV having a black stripe. She would check the number anyway. Then she heard a voice behind her. "Can I help you?" She froze, then turned to come face-to-face with May Simmons.

"I was on my way to see you," she replied. "Tracy and I figured you are alone and may want some company. We thought you might want to join our bubble and come to dinner tomorrow night?"

Keke waited nervously for May's response. The woman's eyes were cold and her jaw was hardened. But in a fraction of a second, May's demeanor shifted. "Oh, that would be lovely," she replied. "I could do with some company. What are you doing now? I don't suppose you would like to come in and share a bottle of wine with me? It's much nicer drinking with some company, don't you think?"

Keke couldn't believe her good luck. She could find out more about this mysterious woman. "I would love to!" she gushed, following May up the pathway to the top of the hill.

# CHAPTER 39

Tracy waited until seven o'clock and then decided to go looking for Keke. She knew her friend should be back by now, having been gone two hours. It was nearly dark and the street was eerily empty of movement. The local shops closed at six o'clock. It was the Thursday before Easter weekend and she knew the police were setting up roadblocks to prevent people from moving out of their communities. It was forbidden for anyone to travel out of their towns and head for their holiday houses. You had to either stay in your holiday bach or permanent residence during lockdown. She presumed there was a roadblock at the entrance to Totara North.

It was a full moon and the street was light enough for her to see in both directions. There was no sign of Keke, and she was not answering her phone. Tracy passed the entrance to the cottage and noticed the lights were flickering through the tree-tops. She wondered if Keke had managed to get the number of the woman's car plate. Tracy continued on around the corner to the boat ramp and jetty. It was completely deserted. No one in sight. She walked out onto the jetty and pulled the collar of her jacket up to shield against the evening's cool breeze. She tried Keke's phone once more. It went straight to voicemail. *She must have her phone off,* thought Tracy. It was really strange. Tracy made her way back to Keke's bed-and-breakfast lodge hoping Keke had returned. She hadn't. It was now eight-thirty and there was no word from her. She checked her phone to see if she had missed a call. Nothing.

When her husband called at nine o'clock, Tracy was beside herself. "Oh, Steve, thank goodness you called. Keke is missing. I can't find her anywhere."

"What do you mean, missing?"

"She went out about five-thirty to check on the woman in the cottage's car and hasn't returned."

"Why would she check on her car?"

"Because she thought it was the same car that belongs to the woman who is missing from the overseas flight. The white Nissan," Tracy explained.

"That woman owns a white Nissan? There are hundreds of them. What made Keke think it belongs to her?"

"You know Keke. She's always trying to make a mystery out of everything. She had seen the woman's mail and said she thought the letters were from banks and the motor vehicle company with new IDs. She's crazy. You know that."

"Is she not answering her phone?" he asked.

"No, it goes straight to voicemail."

"And you have looked for her," Mason confirmed.

"Yes, I've gone down to the jetty where we usually walk. She is nowhere to be seen. I called out to her. The streets are deserted. No one is around."

"Do you want me to come over?" he asked.

"Yes, would you? I think I would sooner be at home with

you. This place is giving me the creeps. Will you see if you can find her? I want to go back home."

"You want to join my bubble?" He chuckled. "See you soon, darling. Don't worry. We'll find her."

Tracy went to pack her bag. She was going home. Totara North was beginning to feel like a haunted village. She couldn't wait to leave.

# CHAPTER 40

Audrey really had no choice. This woman's constant interference had become a problem. She had seen her look at her mail and now she was jotting down the license plate number on her car.

"White wine or champagne?" she called out to Keke, who was admiring the heritage-style kitchen.

"Wine is good," she replied.

The women sat at the kitchen table. Audrey was an expert at playing hostess. She smiled warmly at the woman sitting opposite her. "So Keke, tell me, do you enjoy running your BnB here in this beautiful part of the world?"

"Yes, but with lockdown, I'm worried the business may not survive," Keke said.

"Oh, I am sure we will be out of lockdown in a few weeks. The number of cases have dropped dramatically. I hear only twenty-odd cases today."

"Yes. I hope so. What do you do, May?"

Here it was. Prying. "I am a researcher of bees and flora," she said proudly. "I love my work. It's fascinating and keeps me busy."

"Oh. Where do you usually live?" Keke asked.

"All over the place. Wherever my job takes me," Audrey replied. "Another drink?"

"Just one. I have to get back," Keke said. "Can I take a look around the cottage? It's simply beautiful."

"Go ahead. The owners are selling the cottage fully furnished. There are some beautiful pieces in the lounge and entry hall."

As Keke left the kitchen, Audrey reached up into the overhead cupboard and removed a small vial. She would use a heavier than normal dose. Keke was a big woman and she wanted to make sure she would not be returning home anytime soon.

"Why don't we sit out on the front deck and look at the view," Audrey suggested. "There are blankets out there if we get cold."

"Yes, that would be great." Keke seemed to be enjoying herself, basking in Audrey's attention.

As they sat and sipped the wine, Audrey watched Keke slowly sink into her blanket on the old-fashioned bench seat. The full moon was bright in the sky. The morepork owls hooted their distinctive call in the distance. There was not a human sound.

Audrey sat for quite some time enjoying the stillness of the evening. There was no longer any conversation. Keke had long ago fallen into a deep coma. The poison would take a little longer. Audrey would wait until the early hours of the morning before driving her nosy neighbor to the waterfront. A fall, they would say.

# CHAPTER 41

DC Steve Mason arrived at Keke's to find his wife packed and ready to move home. Tracy was upset. There was no doubt about that. *Damn Keke and her neurotic ways,* he thought. *Where the hell is she?* Together they searched the neighborhood. With a population of only two hundred residents and a sprinkling of homes, he figured she would not be hard to find. Unfortunately, a lot of properties were quite remote and positioned atop the Totara hills. There were side roads leading into darkness. Residents were hiding behind closed doors, afraid of letting people into their homes for fear of infection. Two weeks of isolation had created a population with a certain amount of paranoia. Mason understood this. Knocking on doors would not be the appropriate way to handle the situation. Instead, they searched the streets.

"You don't suppose she fell into the harbor or anything stupid like that?" Tracy asked as they walked along the jetty.

DC Mason shone his torch in the dark waters. "Are you sure she doesn't know someone in the area she could have decided to hang out with?"

"She knows a few people. But people here pretty much keep to themselves. The pub is closed. There is nothing open for miles around here. All I know is she was going to the cottage to check on May's car."

"Okay. I'll go check with her. But you have to stay in the car. I can say it's a neighborhood check on a missing person."

"Thanks, Steve. I love you. I am so sorry to have to get you mixed up in this," Tracy said gratefully.

"Totara North really falls into Andy Patterson's beat. But it won't hurt to do a search while I am here. If we get no response, I'll call him and let him know we have a missing person."

DC Mason parked his car behind May's car at the top of the driveway. Tracy sat in the passenger seat and watched her husband walk up the partly lit path to the cottage.

She looked at the white Nissan car and took a photo of the registration number. Why hadn't she gone with Keke when asked? If she had, maybe they wouldn't be looking for her now.

It didn't take long before her husband returned down the path. As soon as he opened the door Tracy asked, "Well, did you talk to her? What did she say?"

"She seems like a nice lady. Very cordial. Lovely cottage. I asked her if she had seen Keke and she said she had not. She wouldn't open the door, worried about keeping social distancing, and had a scarf wrapped around her face. She sounded very concerned Keke was missing. Said she had met you both before. Of course, she didn't know you were my wife. She said you had come to ask about the cottage being on the market. She hadn't seen Keke since. She said she had taken her usual walk down to the jetty and returned home a few hours ago and has been home all evening," Mason said.

"Let's go back to Keke's and see if she has returned," Tracy suggested.

"Tracy, I don't have much time. We're all on border duty from midnight tonight. We have to set up roadblocks to stop people trying to leave their homes for Easter and heading off to their holiday homes," Mason said gently.

Tracy was still worried. "She would have called me if she was going to be this late."

"Maybe her phone is flat or turned off," Mason suggested.

"Yes, true, she always forgets to charge her phone," Tracy agreed.

To appease his wife, Mason called the Kaeo police station and reported Keke missing. They said they would do a more detailed search in the area. The coastguard could check out the harbor around the jetty and the boat ramp. They suggested Tracy call her family and friends to see if they had heard from her. And they would track her phone to see if she was still in the area.

Mason took Tracy back to Cable Bay, where she could start making calls. "I should have stayed at Keke's in case she returns," Tracy said.

"The police said they would have someone check out her property," Mason said.

"I feel awful," Tracy admitted. "Why didn't I go on the walk with her?"

"Tracy, Andy and his team will find her. She is most likely hanging out with someone and having a good time."

"I hope so," Tracy said.

# CHAPTER 42

I t was almost midnight when Audrey heard the helicopter overhead and saw the coastguard's lights in the harbor. Search lights lit up the hills. *Fuck!* she swore to herself. Disposing of body tonight in the harbor was not going to work. Keeping the body hidden until the search parties left was the only alternative.

There was easy and quick access to the large, square concrete water tank in the backyard. The derelict tank was empty. She filled a bucket with ice and found a crowbar and wheelbarrow in the workspace under the house. When the helicopter moved farther up the road, she took the opportunity to move the body on the trolley to the tank. Using the crowbar to open the lid, she pushed Keke's body through the hole. Pouring ice over the body, she closed the lid. Audrey had read the police helicopters had thermal imaging cameras, and although the water tank had thick walls, she wasn't taking any chances. The body would be kept cold until she could dispose of it in the harbor.

Before she moved the body, she made sure she had turned off all the lights in the cottage. She didn't want the police making another visit. The search seemed to last for hours. Audrey was tired. It had been a long night.

Lying in bed, she stared at the ceiling and thought about Kathy. They had met again earlier in the evening at their usual place. Audrey confided in her she had to find alternative accommodation in a couple of weeks when Level 4 was over as the cottage would be going back on the market. Really, Audrey just wanted to be with Kathy and away from her neighbors, who were proving to be troublesome. She was becoming too conspicuous in the cottage. Her neighbor next door, that Tracy woman who was friends with Keke, and now the police had made two visits to her property. She needed to move her car. Someone may realize she had altered the registration number. Audrey didn't like loose ends.

Kathy's house was tucked away deep in the hills with just a small gravel road for access. It was not visible from the road. With Kathy's current home being California, she had no friends and no other family who would be visiting them after lockdown. It was the perfect place for Audrey to live. Kathy had suggested Audrey stay with her. She had said, "We would love the company. The house is huge. I could use some female company. Dad is a dear, but he's getting old and repeats the same old stories."

Audrey now had to figure out how to dispose of the body before moving to Kathy's house. It would be difficult with the police buzzing around the area. She would just have to wait for the right time.

With that thought, Audrey fell into a deep and peaceful sleep.

# CHAPTER 43

Constable Andrew Patterson headed the search on Easter Friday. Keke Green owned a bed-and-breakfast lodge in Totara North. Forty-five years old, two hundred pounds, dark hair, brown eyes, and last seen taking a walk to a neighbor's house. When Patterson discovered the missing woman was visiting the woman in the cottage, he was curious. Why was she visiting the woman during lockdown? Did she know her?

He had talked to Tracy Mason, DC Mason's wife, who had been staying with her. Tracy had explained Keke wanted to see if the woman's car matched the one she had seen on the TV. Tracy said Keke had become a little obsessed with the woman, whom they now knew was named May Simmons. The police had ruled out she was the missing woman from the flight. She had a similar car and similar appearance to the woman the virus contact team were looking for. But she had shown her passport with her name, along with her driver's license and bank cards. To put it simply, she had ID to prove she was not the missing woman.

Patterson had called on the woman early that morning. She

was wearing a mask and said he could come into the house while she had collected her ID. He had looked around the kitchen. The bedroom French doors were open to the backyard. The terraced garden was overgrown. An old concrete water tank sat in the backyard. When the woman had returned with the IDs, he documented the information and apologized for having to call on her during lockdown. He had already confirmed on previous visits the registration on the car was different and it had an additional black stripe down each side.

The men were still out searching the neighborhood. They had knocked on almost every door in the small village with no success. Keke Green was nowhere to be seen. Keke's car was still parked in her garage. She had left on foot to walk just three-quarters of a mile. The cottage was a stone's throw to the jetty and the boat ramp. Had she fallen in? Jumped in? Did she have personal problems? Her business was closed; money would be running out. Was she depressed? The area of the harbor spanned about seven and half miles, big enough to lose a body.

By sunset there was no sign of Keke and no body had been found. There was a farm in Totara North spreading onto a peninsula. The police helicopter searched the paddocks and the neighboring bush to no avail. The coastguard had searched the shore along the harbor and even across the harbor towards Whangaroa. Nothing.

Tomorrow they would continue the search until the woman was found.

# CHAPTER 44

The story about the missing woman in Totara North was not the main story on the evening news. Covid-19 updates were now a nightly obsession as New Zealanders were shut-in to their homes with just the TV and internet for entertainment. The missing woman, the increase in burglaries, and violence on the streets didn't make the headlines. Keke Green's disappearance seemed to be just another inconvenience during lockdown taking up precious first-responders' time when they could be out dealing with the pandemic.

Audrey had waited until the night searches ceased. She had heard the search would begin again tomorrow morning at first light. She would move the body tonight. The body could easily be hidden amongst the mangrove trees, which provided a dense coverage and muddy floor at the water's edge. Mangrove trees only grew in the top half of New Zealand and thrived in the coastal seawater of the harbor. The challenge would be getting the body down the communal driveway, past her neighbor, and across the street to its final resting place amongst the roots and shoots of the trees. The only way would be in her car. That way, she could take the body farther down the road, closer to where Keke's lodge was located.

Moving two hundred pounds of dead weight was not easy. Thank goodness the lid of the water tank was big enough to enable her to maneuver the large body out of the tank and onto a trolley. She had turned the car around earlier in the day, so the trunk of the car was out of view from the neighbor. Audrey had lined the trunk with a large plastic tarpaulin. With the body tied securely to the trolley, she slowly wheeled her large cargo down the path and into the open trunk. Although slender nowadays, Audrey was always strong. She had learned the easiest way to move large objects—and this was one of her largest. Once in the car she could relax. No one was out on the streets. The police had returned to their pandemic duties of roadblocks on the main motorways during the holiday weekend.

Audrey found the perfect spot. She could dispose of the body out of sight of any passersby. The old sawmill. It had been abandoned for years. She took a side road and parked down by the edge of the water. She had turned off her lights so as not to attract any attention. It was easier than she had expected. The body was heavy and sunk into the dark, muddy ground sheltered by mangroves. She had been thorough in the disposal of the body. Audrey had covered the body with sea water in the water tank so forensics would presume Keke had been in the harbor since she went missing. She was careful to leave Keke's phone on the shore far enough away not to be lost to sea but close enough to be found with the body. On the phone she had included a suicide note.

She returned home and removed the plastic tarpaulin, then went inside and poured a glass of champagne. Life was good. She could now leave the cottage and join Kathy in quiet seclusion.

# CHAPTER 45

Martin heard the sirens. He figured they had found the missing woman. The sirens stopped by the old sawmill. He had not moved out of his bed for days. His cough and fever were worse, and his head ached. He knew he should call his doctor. He had not received word yet about his test. He must not have the virus. They would have notified him by now. He forgot it was Easter weekend and the answerphone said, if it was an emergency, to dial 111. Was it an emergency? After all, he just had the flu. He decided to sleep for another few hours and if he didn't feel any better, he would call for an ambulance.

He couldn't remember how long he had been sick. He knew it was days, but how many? Martin didn't like to share his problems. He could call Jimmy and Poppy but there was nothing they could do. He had his supply of drugs and water by the bed. His sense of taste and smell was non-existent. He knew this was a sign of Covid-19.

The phone by his bed vibrated. He picked it up. It was a call from the community testing service. "Mr. Melrose, your Covid-19 test has come back positive. How are you feeling?"

"I feel like shit!" he replied.

"Are you having difficulty breathing?" the woman on the phone asked.

"No, but I have a dry cough, fever, and bloody awful headache."

"Do you think you can isolate at home?" she asked.

"I don't know," he answered.

"We need to ask you some questions. Is that all right?"

"Go ahead," he replied.

The call lasted some time. He explained he had been in self-isolation for the two weeks' lockdown. The only contact with other people was once with his next-door neighbor, May, and they had shared a few drinks. Yes, she was in her own bubble. No, he didn't know if she had been overseas. No, he knew very little about her except she was looking after the cottage next door as a favor for the owners who lived in Auckland. No, he doesn't have their contact information. He said prior to lockdown he was just working at home on some odd jobs. He had visited the local Mangonui Four Square, Gloss, the Mangonui Lotto store, and been down at the local pub a few times.

They asked for May's phone number but he said didn't have it. When she called, it came up as no caller ID.

The woman said they would follow up with him daily to check on his health. They gave him a number to call if his breathing became difficult or he needed medical help.

Martin could not understand how he had caught the virus. Did May have it? Surely not. He was much too tired to get out of bed. He moaned when he hung up. *Fuck! I feel like shit!*

# CHAPTER 46

When Tracy heard the news, she was horrified. "Found in the harbor by the old mill!" She couldn't believe it. "She said she was just going for a walk to the cottage. How did she end up in the water?"

"There was a suicide note on her phone. Did you know she was that depressed?" Mason asked.

"She wasn't at all depressed. We drank wine every night. We laughed. She was happy. Okay. She was a little obsessed with the woman in the cottage, but you know she loves a good mystery to solve. She thought she may have located the missing woman from the Air New Zealand flight."

"Because it is lockdown, someone has to go and identify the body. I can do it if necessary," he offered.

"She has no family. Her parents passed away a few years ago. I don't think I can do it. I just can't believe it. I know she was worried about her business and her mortgage. But to kill herself? I just can't believe she would do it. Especially to be found in the mud in the mangroves. Poor Keke," Tracy said tearfully.

"You have been through enough. She was your best friend, Trace. You stay here and get some rest."

Tracy knew her husband was busy. The roadblocks were everywhere. But finding Keke's body in the mangroves was something she couldn't get out of her mind. What was her friend doing down by the old sawmill? Keke had to pass by there on the way to the cottage. Had she changed her mind about checking on the car? Or had she planned to kill herself all along?

Tracy started to call Keke's friends. It wasn't easy. How could she tell people that loved her Keke was found in the harbor? There would an autopsy, but it was pretty obvious it had been a suicide. There was no sign of any bruising or violence of any kind, her husband had said.

Only one person could attend a funeral during lockdown. Who would it be?

# CHAPTER 47

Audrey was packed and ready to depart the little cottage. It was a shame she had to leave. If it wasn't for all the bloody busybodies knocking at her door or peering over the fence, she could have stayed here. At least until lockdown was over. But she really had no choice. She washed her coffee cup and put it away. She would miss sitting at the table in the kitchen, sipping wine on the balcony overlooking the boats and sparkling water, watching the sunrise and the sunset from atop the Totara hills. She had been thorough, wiping every surface she ever touched. She could not afford to leave her DNA anywhere. She replaced the key under the flowerpot and walked down the now-familiar pathway to her car. Placing her suitcase in the back seat, she backed down the driveway, made a turn, and headed toward the jetty and on to Kathy's hidden homestead, past the old store and down the gravel road.

This morning she had been woken by sirens and knew they had found the body. She had hoped it would take a day or two before it was found. It meant she had to move a little sooner than later. She had called Kathy and said she really didn't want to be alone with all the police activity and the poor woman found close by in the harbor. Kathy had told her to come immediately.

Kathy was waiting for her when Audrey pulled into their driveway. She led the way through the old French doors to the main living room and up a flight of stairs to a beautiful bedroom overlooking the water.

"There is a bathroom next door," Kathy explained. "You have your own space up here. Dad and I sleep on the next level. I told you the house is huge. I am so happy you are staying here."

"I am happy to be here," Audrey said. "I must admit, it was a little lonely by myself. I'm grateful for the company."

"This Covid-19 has us all on edge, and with the poor woman's body found in the harbor by the old sawmill this morning, it makes you wonder why all this is happening now. I hear there are twenty cases of the virus in Northland. I wish I knew where. Hopefully we don't have any cases up here in the far north."

"Did you know the woman who drowned?" Audrey asked.

"My father knew her. She hadn't been here long. But I heard she was a nice woman. Ran one of the bed-and-breakfast lodges down by the old museum. First-class accommodation. The lodge was built in the early 1900s, like your friends' cottage. I wonder what happened? The police called on us the night before to ask if we had seen her. We hadn't, of course. But I'll let you settle in and unpack. Come on down to the lounge when you're ready; we can have a glass of wine and watch the sunset."

Audrey replaced the sim card in her burner phone. A new beginning, she thought. She had left no forwarding address. The cottage would now be vacant. She had not seen or heard from Martin. She had noticed his curtains had been closed for days.

His car was still parked outside his house, so she presumed he was home.

It was almost midnight when flashing lights headed up the driveway to Martin's house. He had called the ambulance. He couldn't catch his breath. He had no choice.

# CHAPTER 48

Jimmy Bromley received the message a new Covid-19 case had been confirmed in Totara North. When he reviewed the information, he was shocked to learn it was his good friend, Martin Melrose. "Poppy," he called. "Poppy, Martin has just been taken to intensive care with Covid-19."

"Oh, no! That's terrible!" Poppy said.

"This is the first case that has been hospitalized in Northland. Most are self-isolating or have recovered. But for some reason, they're having difficulty tracing his contacts." He knew Martin had been diligent by keeping in lockdown for the past sixteen days. Even before lockdown, he had been in self-isolation.

"He must have caught it from the woman in the cottage. May? Isn't that her name?" Poppy replied.

"We will need to test her. Poor Martin. He finally finds a nice woman and she gives him Covid-19. How is his luck?"

Bromley was concerned for his good friend. He was in his sixties, but it was consoling to know he was a fit guy. Still, he shook his head. *Damn.*

His office sent over Martin's phone records. He recognized

his phone number, and an unlisted number which he presumed was his neighbor's. Both made within the last two weeks. There were a few identified numbers, mostly local businesses.

WHEN BROMLEY ARRIVED IN TOTARA NORTH, THE cottage was empty. No sign of May or her car. He knocked a few times and looked in the windows. The cottage seemed clean and well maintained. He could see why Poppy wanted to buy this place. He took his time and walked up the front steps to the balcony, where he could look into an entrance hall. Some curtains were shut. The house was full of furniture; he presumed it was being sold fully furnished. Surely May had not furnished the place for just a few weeks' visit.

He returned to the back entrance, which led up the terraced paths to the back boundary and a small water holding tank. Another big, ancient concrete water tank was nearby. If they bought the cottage. he would need to check on the water supply. The gardens were overgrown. He knew Poppy loved to garden. He would contact the real estate agent and see if she could give him May's phone number. He might even put in an offer on the place.

He figured May could not be far away. She had taken her car, but with the travel restrictions, she could have only gone out for essential supplies. The nearest shop was in Mangonui. There was also a Kaeo Four Square. Either way, she would be back in less than an hour. In the meantime, he would take a trip down to the wharf and boat ramp. If they lived here, he would buy a small boat.

Bromley drove to the site of the old sawmill, where a woman's body had been found in the mangroves. The area was roped off. It was only a few minutes' walk from the boat ramp and jetty. Three years ago, when he was Detective Constable Bromley, he would have been right on top of this case. Seemed as though Totara North was in the news quite a lot these days. Old Luke Street had passed away just a couple of weeks ago, now this woman who owned a local bed-and-breakfast lodge was found drowned in the harbor, and to top it off, Covid-19 had penetrated this quiet harborside village. The situation reminded him of three years ago, when deaths became the norm in Hihi. Audrey Wetherby, the woman who was responsible for so many murders, had been living in plain sight. By the time they had figured out she was responsible, she had simply disappeared, slipped through their fingers. Bromley had to admit he was beginning to miss his old job. Steve Mason now had his job. He was a good man.

The old pub was deserted. All pubs in New Zealand were closed during lockdown. Shame, he would have liked a beer while he was waiting for May to return. He looked at the time. She had been gone now for forty-five minutes. He returned to the cottage and waited. There were no other neighbors in close proximity to Martin's house. He had checked the area. Old man Luke owned the surrounding land and he was dead. Martin and May lived on small quarter-acre lots adjoining the old man's property.

Bromley waited for over an hour to no avail. He left a note for May to contact him urgently, explaining her neighbor, Martin, had been confirmed with Covid-19 and she needed to get tested immediately for her own safety and that of others. He left his phone number, along with information pertaining to the testing facilities in the area. He also asked her to register online with the District Health Board.

His next trip would be to the local Four Square shops, the only other two sources of contact made by Martin prior to lockdown. They knew from overseas reports the pumps at the petrol stations also were a possible source of contamination. But, as no other case had been reported in the local area, Bromley could only surmise it must have come from Martin's neighbor, May.

When he returned home, he called the agent who had listed the cottage, Rose Bright. She could not provide any information on May. However, she did provide the owners' contact information. He tried calling. There was no answer, so he left a message.

# CHAPTER 49

It was day seventeen of lockdown. Two more deaths had been reported, totaling four deaths in total. Only twenty-nine new cases were announced, making a total of 1,312 infected to date. Four hundred and forty-two cases had recovered. More were recovering than were getting infected. It was a good sign. Detective Constable Mason hoped things would get back to normal by May. Easter weekend had been a lot quieter than expected. The roads were almost empty of traffic. Road-blocks had deterred the holiday travelers from heading to their baches. Normally the far north was one of the busiest holiday locations, with its beaches and warmer climate. Covid-19 had changed all of that.

Mason had been working with the Kaeo police on the death of Keke Green. Tracy was so adamant she had not taken her own life, and he had convinced the forensics team to do a comprehensive autopsy to determine if there was any other cause. Maybe she was taking antidepressant medication that had caused her to get disoriented.

When he received a call from his ex-colleague Jimmy Bromley

to ask if he had any information on the woman living in the cottage below Old Luke's place, he said he had talked to her but, no, he didn't have her phone number. He was surprised to hear her neighbor had been confirmed with Covid-19.

When he asked his wife about it, Tracy said she and Keke had met May's neighbor at the jetty. They had been careful to keep their distance. "He was wearing a mask when we saw him," she said. "We just called out to say hello. We noticed he removed his mask afterwards. Guess he saw we were not wearing one and decided to take his off. Who knows? That is awful. I wonder how he got it?"

"You were not close enough to get infected?"

"Don't worry, we were at least twenty yards away," she replied.

"Jimmy Bromley is working with the District Health Board's contact tracing," he told her. "He is trying to find the contact information for May from the cottage. He called up there but said she was nowhere to be found."

"I know her name, Keke told me. It is May A. Simmons. I remember because Keke thought it was a coincidence her middle name started with an 'A.' She thought it might be Audrey, and you know how obsessed she was with Audrey Wetherby. I also took a photo of her car registration number because Keke was so sure it was the car that belonged to that woman off the Air New Zealand flight." Tracy looked through the photos on her phone and sent the plate number photo to her husband's phone.

"Great. I will send the info to Jimmy." He looked over at his wife. "You are becoming quite a detective yourself," he said.

# CHAPTER 50

A udrey settled into her new lockdown abode. It was strange sharing a home with other people. Her personality of an introvert/extravert combined with being a fully functioning psychopath suited a lifestyle of singular living. Her plans to stay in the cottage had been jeopardized by a multitude of unfortunate situations including, but not limited to, the fact that her next-door neighbor was friends with Poppy and Jimmy Bromley. Of course, being on the Covid-19 tracing hotlist was regrettable to say the least. Getting her and her car out of sight from inquisitive neighbors was her first focus. Now she could concentrate on why she had returned to New Zealand.

She had hidden it in the grounds of Tiromoana in Hihi. A large amount of cash she had stashed away over the years. Her quick departure three years ago did not allow time for her to deposit the money into a bank account or convert it into a saleable asset. She was hoping to launder it through buying real estate but in the past year the New Zealand government had tightened up its anti-money-laundering laws. Now it was almost impossible to buy land without extensive IDs and proof of residency. Buying property with cash would be a definite no-no. Her new passport, driver's license, and bank cards were a start to proving her legitimacy. She just needed a permanent place of residency in order to obtain a utility bill. She had just purchased broadband in the cottage and would receive an invoice in the mail any day now. Unfortunately, it would be mailed to the cottage.

She had been doing online research to educate herself on bees and their effect on native flora. Kathy's dad would ask her questions on the subject at dinner. He seemed genuinely interested. She thought she had chosen an extremely boring profession, but obviously not to an eighty-two-year-old man living in the bush in Totara North.

Kathy was continuously curious about Audrey's background as well. It was becoming difficult to sidestep her many questions. As much as she liked Kathy, if it got too complicated here, she knew she may have to make some changes.

Audrey didn't risk taking a trip to Hihi over Easter weekend. She would wait until mid-week. Hihi was just ten minutes from Mangonui. She could easily be going to shop for groceries. However, getting on the property at Tiromoana would not be easy. It was a private property on the peninsula overlooking Doubtless Bay. She had owned it before leaving for the USA. The new owner was Mei Wong; Audrey had sold her the business rather rapidly before her departure. Mei had since turned the humble, self-contained cabin resort into a five-star luxury resort by combining her hundred-acre property next door with Audrey's ten acres. Audrey presumed the resort would be closed during lockdown with hopefully just a skeleton staff. Maybe only Mei would be on the property.

No one could know she was back in New Zealand, including Mei. She had no idea that Audrey was responsible for a stream of local murders. Audrey would have to approach the property from the waterfront. Tiromoana had multiple accesses to the harbor shoreline. It would be too difficult at night and she would have to walk over a mile along the rocky waterfront and it was only accessible when the tide was out. Her only other option was to wait until dark, make her way up the peninsula on foot, access the property by the main driveway, and hope she could keep in the shadows.

"Dinner's ready!" She heard Kathy calling from the dining room. *Great,* she thought. *Another evening of bloody bees and flora.*

# CHAPTER 51

Jimmy Bromley looked at the latest Covid-19 case numbers on day seventeen of lockdown.

Total of new cases of Covid-19: 18
Total number of recovered cases: 471
Total number of Covid-19 cases to date: 1330
Total number of deaths: 4
Total number of cases related to existing cases: 47%
Total number of cases related to overseas travel: 40%
Total number of tests to date: 61,167
Total number of cases in Northland: 25

He knew there would be more cases in Northland if he couldn't locate her. Her name was May Audrey Simmons. He had the registration number of her car and her address. He did not, however, have her phone number and was concerned he had not heard from her. He called the local testing stations at Kaeo and Kaitaia to see if she had taken his advice and gotten a Covid-19 test. They had no record of her.

State Highway 10 was eerily devoid of traffic. It was Easter Sunday. Everyone was spending this usually social occasion at home in their individual bubbles. Churches were forced to become virtual broadcasters. The prime minister, Jacinda Ardern, had announced during her daily Covid-19 press event the Easter Bunny and the Tooth Fairy were both essential businesses, much to the relief of over six hundred thousand New Zealand children under the age of ten.

It only took fifteen minutes to reach the Totara North junction. The main road was deserted. Arriving at the cottage, he noticed May Simmons's car was not in the carport, indicating she was not at home again. When he approached the back door, he saw his card was still in the crack of the door. *She has not been home,* he surmised. *Where the hell is she?* Residents were supposed to stay put in the place they were when lockdown began. Ms. Simmons obviously had broken those rules. *Maybe she has boyfriend and she is staying with him,* he thought. *Or friends.* He put an alert out on her car. A white Nissan, registration number: OIB188.

He called DC Mason. "Can you run a check on registration number 0IB188?" he said. "Just want to confirm it belongs to May Simmons."

"You haven't located her yet?" Mason asked.

"No, she's not home and her car is gone. Hasn't been back for over twenty-four hours. I thought the car may belong to a boyfriend and I can track where she may have gone."

"Nope, nothing is coming up under that number. Are you sure it's the right number?" Mason said.

"That is the number you gave me," Bromley said.

"That is strange. Very strange. You got the photo Tracy took?" DC Mason said, confused.

"Yes, I am looking at the phone now. OIB188," he confirmed.

"Then I have no idea. We'll keep an eye out for it. She has to go food shopping at some stage."

"Thanks, mate."

Bromley looked at the photo of the car and it triggered a memory. Looked just like the Nissan car that belonged to Anna Ward from the Air New Zealand flight he was tracing. *No. It can't be the same car*, he thought. He checked his notes. CTP133. He looked a little closer at the photo Tracy had taken. Had the number been altered? *Fuck!* He took out a pen and checked. *It is the same fucking car!* Questions flooded his mind. Why would she change the registration number? Why the hell was May Simmons driving Anna Ward's car? Were they friends? Was Ms. Simmons staying with Anna Ward? Where were they? And worse, were they spreading Covid-19 to unsuspecting residents of the far north?

# CHAPTER 52

Easter Sunday was like every other day for Audrey. She wasn't a religious person and had given up eating chocolate years ago. Her mood was becoming dark. She recognized the signs of restlessness that came with the need to finish a project. She had returned home to New Zealand with one, and only one purpose: to collect her cash and invest in a secluded property in the rural far north where she could live comfortably until the borders opened again and she could choose where in the world she would go. She was frustrated with having to share her time and space with Kathy and her dad. She was beginning to feel trapped.

Her car was another problem. It was too dangerous with the cops looking for her. She needed to dump it somewhere where it would not be found.

"I'm just going out for a walk," she called out to Kathy. "Won't be too long." She left before Kathy could reply.

Audrey walked down the narrow gravel road that hugged the shore of the harbor toward the remote hills in the distance until she found the ideal location to drive her car into the bay. It was secluded and remote enough that she felt confident it would not be found. She would need to do this tonight after Kathy and her father were asleep. Rather than explain where her car was, she would simply use theirs.

Upon her return, Kathy presented her with a basket of mini chocolate eggs. "They are the best," she said. "Taste them"

Audrey took a bite, feeling the cold liquid filling explode in her mouth. Fuck! It tasted good.

"Didn't I say? Aren't they the best?"

"The best," said Audrey. "I can't remember the last time I ate chocolate. I forgot how bloody good it is." She took another. "They are addictive."

She watched as Kathy helped herself. "I can't stop eating them," she said.

Audrey knew what she needed to do.

# CHAPTER 53

Constable Patterson had received the autopsy report from the Keke Green case. There was a troubling fact: Ms. Green had no sign of seawater in her lungs when she died. She was dead before entering the water, and the only injuries she appeared to have were numerous scratches, which the coroner presumed were caused by the sharp roots of the mangrove trees. She was only in her late forties, overweight but healthy, based on her recent medical records. There was no sign of antidepressants or any other prescriptive drug. The reason for her death was inconclusive.

He asked for a more comprehensive analysis of anything she could have eaten. He was not prepared to release the body until a toxicology report was carried out. Blood, urine, and hair analysis. There had to be some explanation for the poor woman's untimely death.

He called Rose. He had not talked to her since their dinner date. She was a great cook. She said they would have to share a collective bubble now.

"Rose, what are you doing tonight?" He could hear her

clanging away in the background. "What are you doing?" he asked.

"Oh, hi, Andy. Nice to hear your voice." She laughed. "I am cleaning out my saucepan cupboard. What else am I supposed to do? Either cleaning, working, or eating." She paused. "Tonight? Let me think. Oh yes, I will be cleaning, working, or eating."

"I don't suppose I could join you with the eating part of that scenario? I could bring wine so we could drink, cook, and eat for a little variety."

"I would love you to. I haven't been out to shop for days. Can you pick up a couple of steaks and some wine?"

"No problem. I will see you about seven?"

"Yes, seven is perfect. See you then." She paused. "Oh, and Andy?"

"Yes?"

"I really enjoyed the other night," she said.

"I did too."

# CHAPTER 54

Audrey looked over at her two roommates. They appeared to be sleeping peacefully but, of course, they were dead. Dead as dead could be. She had injected the poison into the center of the Easter eggs and watched as they ate one after the other until the bowl was completely empty. Addictive, they certainly were. Audrey had pleaded an upset stomach after not eating sugar for years. "My body must have reacted badly to the sugar intake," she had explained.

She sat watching the evening news. Covid-19 was infecting the world at an amazing pace with 1,780,356 total cases worldwide and over 100,000 deaths. It had penetrated 210 countries. Her recent tally of deaths was minuscule when you considered the big picture.

When she first saw Kathy, she realized they not only had a lot in common, but they looked very similar: they were both petite, the same height, and the same hair coloring, even similar features. Kathy had different taste in clothes, but that was easily remedied. Audrey would simply change her style.

She left them sitting on the sofa and wandered into Kathy's

bedroom. Opening the wardrobe, she began to sort through the clothes. Kathy wore brighter colors than she did. Reds, blues, yellows, and pinks. Bright scarves, tailored jackets and trousers, expensive shoes, and an obviously lacking collection of hats. Audrey loved hats. Maybe adding a hat or two wouldn't hurt.

It would be no use disposing of Kathy and the car in one location. A DNA check would soon identify the body and they would know it was neither Anna Ward nor May Simmons, as both women did not exist. She would have to dispose of their bodies on the grounds of the secluded property. Audrey was not one for digging graves in the backyard. But there were two big concrete water tanks on the property. It would take a long time to find the bodies in one of them—if they were ever found at all.

In the meantime, she would simply take the identity of Kathy Lane. She found Kathy's passport and California driver's license and studied Kathy's hair and makeup. It would only take a few changes to her own appearance to be easily mistaken for her.

Audrey had a busy night ahead of her. First, she would dispose of the car and walk back to the house. Then she would go to work on emptying one of the tanks and turning off the connection to the house. The thought of drinking contaminated water was not a pleasant one.

# CHAPTER 55

Martin felt like shit. They had put him in intensive care. Thank God he didn't need a respirator.

He had no idea where he had contracted Covid-19. Could have been on a bloody door handle, a food packet, a paint tin from the hardware store. He didn't bloody care. He just wanted to stop feeling so awful. They were giving him oxygen when he needed it. He was determined to recover. He was not going to be a death statistic. Over 80 percent of cases would recover. Only a very small percentage would die. The staff at the hospital were wonderful. One nurse in particular was hot. Well, she looked hot through all the protective gear. He wished he had enough energy to come on to her. He didn't.

No one could visit him in the hospital. No visitors allowed. He had his iPad and phone with him. He had tried to have a conversation with Jimmy, but it was pretty one-sided. Jimmy told him the woman in the cottage was friends with the woman from the Air New Zealand flight and that must have been how he contracted the virus. "May Simmons must have infected you," he said. "Trouble is, we cannot locate her or her friend. She's not at the cottage, hasn't been there for a couple of days. She didn't talk about any of her friends, I suppose?"

Martin was too tired to respond.

"Sorry, man. Get better, okay? Talk soon. Take care."

All Martin could think was, *Fuck May! Fuck all women!*

# CHAPTER 56

A udrey drove down the dirt road with her lights off, with only the moonlight to show the way. No one would be out at this time of night. She had already removed the registration plates and any form of identification on the car. The road ran close to the edge of the bay. There was a vacant bach with a boat ramp. It was surprisingly easy to let the car roll forward into the dark, deep water. She left the windows down, so it filled quickly and disappeared out of sight. No one would be visiting their bach during lockdown. She looked to see if any lights were on in the houses across the bay. It was dark. Silent. She was in no hurry returning to the house. This was the last night she would be May Audrey Simmons. Tomorrow she would be known as Kathy Lane, a conveyancer from California. Of course, she would give notice. She had no plans to return to her old job.

Water tanks. Audrey was grateful most homes in the rural far north had no choice but to use one. Their only source of water was rainwater, caught from roof spouting and piped into water tanks. Audrey was a water tank snob, preferring concrete tanks to plastic tanks. The water purified in the concrete tanks, whereas the water in plastic tanks tasted stale from the heat of the sun. She was pleased there were two large concrete tanks at the property. Even better, they were easy to access as they were positioned on the side of the hill, making it easy to lift the lid and deposit her housemates inside.

The house was nice and quiet when she opened the front door. She placed her house keys on the small round table in the hallway and removed her shoes. She chose to make Kathy's room her own. It had the best view. Plus, it meant she didn't have to exchange wardrobes. A large mirror hung on the wall. Audrey tried on a few different outfits. Her new short black hairstyle accentuated her green eyes. The bright colors would take some getting used to. Audrey had always preferred to wear black. She had to admit the colors were more cheerful and she was feeling particularly cheerful now that she could relax. No more nosy neighbors, she didn't have to worry about her car, and she had her privacy back. It had been a very productive day.

Tomorrow she would wear red and drive the old man's Ute to Hihi. She had a new identity and a home to call her own. All she needed was her money.

# CHAPTER 57

DC Mason set up a roadblock on State Highway 10 south of Doubtless Bay. The beaches within the next ten miles were popular holiday spots. It was Easter Monday and he knew people would be getting restless as New Zealand headed into its third week of lockdown.

The traffic was light. As he pulled over vehicles heading north, he heard excuses of every kind. "Just visiting my sick aunt" was the excuse of a group of twenty-somethings with surfboards tied to the roof of their car. "Can't find the coffee I like in the local dairy so off to Kaitaia's Pak'nSave." A forty-minute drive to get coffee was not acceptable.

An old black Ute was indicating to turn into Hihi Road. He waved the woman over. "Do you live in Hihi?" he asked the women in red. "Can I see your driver's license?"

"I'm visiting my girlfriend, who also lives alone. We are sharing our bubbles," she explained as she handed the officer her driver's license.

"Who is your friend?" he asked as he checked the warrant and registration.

"Mei Wong, at the Tiromoana Resort," she replied.

"Your warrant has expired," he said.

"Oh, I am sorry. Can't get it renewed in lockdown," she explained.

"I know Mei Wong," he said. "Give her my regards, Ms. Lane," he said, returning her license.

"I will."

The woman was dressed to kill. Quite stunning. She wore a red scarf wrapped around her head and across her face. Dark glasses hid her eyes. Something about her was familiar. Kathy Lane . . . she lived in Totara North, it said on her license. He jotted down the registration number of her vehicle. It was dirty and looked like it had spent most of its life being driven off-road. It was a stark comparison to the sophisticated woman driving it. DC Mason had a nose for those things. *Maybe it's her partner's Ute,* he thought.

It was quiet. He decided to call in the registration number of the Ute. It belonged to Matt Lane. Must be her partner.

He looked at the time. It was getting on to noon. He decided to drive into Hihi and make sure no one was out fishing or boating in the bay.

As he passed Hihi Beach and headed on up the peninsula, he saw the black Ute parked down a track to the beach. Why had the woman parked there rather than park up at the resort? Mei was a good friend of Tracy's, and Mason and his wife had spent many happy hours at the resort. He had meant to check on Mei during lockdown. No time like the present.

The resort was really quiet. Mei had opened up the resort for health workers so there were a few cabins that were obviously occupied. He pulled up outside the main office and saw it was closed. He drove a mile up the private road to her large home overlooking the bay. Mei lived there with her new partner, Geoff. He saw them sitting outside on their deck.

"Steve," Mei called out. "Nice to see you."

"Hi, Mei. Hi, Geoff. I just ran into your friend, Kathy Lane, heading into Hihi and she reminded me I haven't seen you guys since lockdown. Just checking all is okay."

"Who?" asked Mei.

"Kathy Lane. She said was heading out to see you. I think she said 'to share your bubble.'"

"I have no idea who Kathy Lane is," Mei said. "Do you, Geoff?"

"Nope, never heard of her," Geoff replied.

"Maybe it's someone wanting to stay at the resort. But we are closed to the public," Mei said.

"I saw her car parked at the bottom of your land at the track to the beach,"

Mason added, standing the required distance.

"That is strange," Mei said. "Maybe she's fishing down on the shore."

"She wasn't dressed for fishing," Mason said. "Never mind. Have a great day. Nice to see you both. Keep safe."

As he passed the track, the Ute was gone. *Strange,* he thought. He just couldn't get out of his mind that she sounded familiar. *Where have I heard that voice before?*

When he got home, he checked where Kathy and Matt Lane lived in Totara North. Maybe that would jog his memory. It didn't.

# CHAPTER 58

The results came back from the lab. Keke Green had tested positive for oleander poisoning, and her hair showed she possibly had GHB in her system. The effects of GHB only lasts up to eight hours in the blood and up to twelve hours in urine, but hair tests although less accurate for detecting GHB, can offer a much longer detection window of up to one month. The results showed there was a possible positive GHB result in Keke's hair.

Where had Patterson heard of this combination before? Why had Keke consumed both GHB and oleander? GHB was known as a date drug, but a heavy dose can cause death. Meanwhile, the oleander plant was a known poison. The coroner had confirmed death by poison.

After a search in the police files, he read there had been quite a few cases of oleander poisoning in the north. Many were linked to a serial murderer, Audrey Wetherby. Yes, that was where he had heard of it. Audrey Wetherby had lived in Whangaroa and later in Hihi. By the time the police had figured out she was responsible for a stream of murders in the area, she had disappeared. Was she back again? He pulled up a photo of the woman. Blonde, in her fifties maybe. He didn't recognize her. He checked her last known address. It was the Tiromoana Resort in Hihi. His mind raced. *Holy shit!* he thought. Did he have a serial killer on his hands? There was no doubt in his mind that Keke Green's death was homicide. Poisoned.

He wrote up his report and send it in to headquarters. He sent a copy to DC Mason in the Mangonui station. Maybe he could check out the resort in Hihi just to make sure everything was okay. If Audrey Wetherby had returned to the area, she may revisit her familiar hangouts.

He was having dinner with Rose tonight. He turned out the lights in the station and walked down to his car. Kaeo was quiet. The dairy was still open but there were only a few shoppers in the store. The two petrol stations in the town were deserted. People were staying home.

# CHAPTER 59

F*uck!* Audrey swore to herself. She realized it was too late to turn around without causing suspicion. The cop car was parked at the entrance to Hihi Road. She had already indicated to turn right when she saw his car. He pulled her over. She tightened the scarf around her face. She had seen him before. He had come to the cottage and questioned her about Keke. Thank goodness for Covid-19 and the excuse to wear face protection. He asked for her license and she handed him Kathy's license. He had asked her why she was heading into Hihi. She knew there were no shops there and no one was allowed to visit beaches; all she could think of was Mei. He said he knew her. That wasn't good. But she had no choice—she had to drive into Hihi.

She parked her car off the road, hoping it was out of sight of the main beach. She walked down the track to the rocky shore. The tide was in. There was no way she could walk around the shoreline to Tiromoana even if she wanted to. She sat on the rocks and looked out at the bay. She used to own this property. It was only ten acres then. Now Mei owned a hundred and ten acres. Audrey had not seen the new resort. Fancy, she had heard it was. Spa, tennis courts, swimming pool, luxury lodges, cabins, and cabanas down on the new sandy beach. When Audrey had moved there, it just consisted of a small cottage and a cabin. She had added a few more cabins but it was pretty basic. The rocky beach bought back many memories. Some good, some not so good.

As she was returning to the Ute, she saw a police car heading up the peninsula towards Tiromoana. She hid behind the tall bamboo beside the track and watched as he disappeared around the corner. *He is going to Mei's,* she realized. *Shit!* She waited until he was out of sight, returned to the old ugly Ute, and headed back to Totara North. Coming to Hihi had not been a good idea. She would need to wait or come up with an alternative plan.

# CHAPTER 60

DC Mason read the message from Andy Patterson in shock. Was Audrey Wetherby back in town? Who else would use GHB and oleander? The only reason forensics had checked for this combination was because it was the infamous Ms. Wetherby's known weapon of choice. Ever since she'd been active, any suspicious death in the far north involving a toxicology must include both GHB and oleander.

He looked at the photo of her. Blonde, buxom, friendly-looking woman. Although he had not been working in the far north during her reign of murders, he and everyone else on the force had followed the case. The Bromleys would be interested to learn of the Keke case findings. But Bromley was no longer part of the police force; he did private investigative work now. This file was active and confidential. Totara North was not in DC Mason's jurisdiction, but he felt personally responsible for finding out what, and possibly who, had caused his wife's best friend death. He didn't want Tracy to know Keke could possibly have been murdered. Had she taken the combination of GHB and oleander herself for a suicide? That was the most obvious answer. After all, she was obsessed with Audrey Wetherby.

He made a note to Constable Patterson suggesting Ms. Keke Green may well have taken the concoction herself due to her obsession with Audrey Wetherby. He said she had a copy of Poppy Bromley's book with information on GHB and oleander poisoning and had been obsessing over the Audrey murders, as they were known, in the past few weeks. He suggested Constable Patterson look through Keke's belongings for anything relating to Audrey Wetherby. He was sure he would find proof of the woman's fixation on the case.

But what if Audrey Wetherby had returned to the far north? Was it just a coincidence that only today he had visited her last known location? DC Mason didn't believe in coincidences.

# CHAPTER 61

Audrey knew she couldn't risk being seen in Hihi in daylight again. She would have to wait until dark. Upon returning to the villa she checked out her reflection in the mirror. She did look completely different from all her past identities. Her short black pageboy hairstyle, different makeup, slender body, bright clothing, and her changed demeanor no longer belonged to the infamous Audrey Wetherby. The only aspect of herself she couldn't change was her DNA.

A search in old Matt Lane's room found his bank details. The sooner she could deposit her money safely in his account, the happier she would be. She could then transfer the money into Kathy's account and on to an overseas offshore account, which she had already set up. Easy for the bank to understand the old man didn't trust banks and had kept his money under his mattress, so to speak.

But with the country in lockdown and only frontliners such as hospital staff and emergency services allowed out in the middle of the night, she would need to create a diversion if she was ever going to get close to her money.

She made the phone call to the Mangonui police station at ten-thirty advising them of a group gathering taking place in the outskirts of Taipa near Peria. Sounds like a large party, she had said. They sound drunk. At least forty or fifty people. No, she didn't want to give her name. She was worried about them knowing she reported them. Audrey had used a rough kiwi accent. She replaced the sim card immediately after placing the call. She would have to leave immediately. Fifteen minutes to get to Hihi and it would take some time to retrieve her cash. She just prayed Mei was already in bed over at her house and that the resort had no guests.

# CHAPTER 62

DC Mason was enjoying a quiet night before getting a call to say there was a big party going on in the outbacks of Taipa. Shit! The woman had not given an address and Peria was in the middle of nowhere. He passed the refuse center and continued down a narrow gravel road into the abyss. He came to the fork in the road: one way led to Kaitaia, the other farther into the countryside. He saw no lights, heard no noise—it was deathly quiet. Maybe the party had closed down. Unlikely, as it was still early, only eleven. Parties out here went on to the wee hours of the morning. He kept driving until he figured the gathering had gotten word the police been called on them. Or it was just a prank call. He turned around and drove back to the Taipa shopping center on the main highway. He parked and pulled over traffic to enquire why they were out in the middle of the night during lockdown. Some were shift workers at Kaitaia Hospital, others were breaking the rules. He gave warnings to some and fines to others.

He thought about the Keke Green case. He had decided he

would tell Tracy before she heard it on the news. Keke Green had been poisoned. He knew his wife would be horrified. He also knew, as a good reporter for the local paper, she would want to know as much as he could tell her. Knowing her, she would be tenacious in gathering background information. Patterson had called him to say they were announcing the cause of Keke's death on tomorrow morning's news.

When he arrived home, Tracy was waiting up for him. He told her as much as he could.

When he finished, Tracy's eyes were wide. "Keke was right! She suspected that Audrey Wetherby was back. I should have listened to her. She would not have taken her own life."

DC Mason didn't get much sleep that night. His wife wanted to know everything about the Audrey murders. By dawn, she had written her article, which would appear online and in the newspaper tomorrow.

Photos of Keke Green and Audrey Wetherby accompanied the headline.

"MURDER IN THE FAR NORTH! IS AUDREY BACK IN TOWN?"

*The body of Keke Green was found on Easter Friday in the mangroves on the water's edge in Totara North. The coroner has confirmed her death as caused by a combination of GHB and oleander poisoning. Ms. Green was known in the area for her interest in the Audrey murders that took place in the far north between 2012 and 2017. Her decision to purchase a bed-and-breakfast lodge in Totara North was influenced by Audrey Wetherby's ownership of two similar businesses during her reign of murder. Ms. Green had suspected Audrey Wetherby was back in the area. It is well-known Ms. Wetherby's choice of weapon was the same combination of GHB and oleander poisoning. Police have not ruled out suicide; however, there is an ongoing search for the truth.*

# CHAPTER 63

This time Audrey had no problem driving to Hihi. She parked her car farther down the track to the beach where it could not be spotted from the road. The streets were completely empty all the way from Totara North to the small seaside village. As she walked up the winding gravel road toward Tiromoana, she stayed in the shadows on the edge of the road. It was about half a mile up the peninsula to the entrance of Tiromoana. Audrey had not been back since the day she left for America. She had heard Mei had upgraded the property into the five-star resort and was eager to see the result. Reaching the gate, she was horrified to see the acres of tall pine trees had been felled. The once private driveway edged with seventy-foot pines was completely exposed. Her silhouette in the moonlight would be visible for miles around. Fuck! She stopped at the entrance for a moment to consider her options. Mei's house was on the next ridge a mile away. The old cottage and surrounding cabins were straight ahead. She would take the risk.

As Audrey approached the entrance to the resort, she was relieved to see Mei had kept the native bush and trees. A new swimming pool and tennis courts were solar-lit, so Audrey hid in the shadows. More cabins had been added to the resort. As she reached the front lawn where her cottage had sat overlooking the bay, she froze. Fuck! It was gone! The area was now an outside dining restaurant with tables and chairs covered by a large canvas awning.

This was a problem. Her money had been buried in the floor of the old shed attached to the cottage. Never for one moment did she think the building would be demolished. A large serving counter had replaced the old shed. The ground was now covered in concrete paving stones. She had no option. She could not access her money tonight. She sat at one of the tables and looked over the bay in the moonlight. Such memories of her years spent here. At first, she had been horrified at having to live here when she had lost her fortune, but time heals all wounds and she had turned the property into a successful business.

The night was cool and a southwesterly wind was blowing across the bay. She pulled her hood up on her jacket and looked out at sea. The half-moon was shrouded in high clouds.

Then a voice broke the silence and a light blinded her eyes. "Can I help you?"

Audrey turned to see a man standing only six feet from her shining a light directly into her face.

# CHAPTER 64

Jimmy and Poppy Bromley were sitting at the breakfast table searching online for everything they could find about Keke Green's death.

"You don't think she's back?" Poppy looked at her screen, completely transfixed.

"She wouldn't dare. She would be recognized immediately."

"A woman can change her appearance. She could look completely different."

"But why? Why would she risk it?" Bromley wasn't convinced.

"Who knows? Who knows why she murders? She doesn't live by reason."

"It sounds, from reading Tracy's article, like Keke Green was obsessed with Audrey Wetherby. It's more likely she killed herself using the same method as Audrey Wetherby used to kill most of her victims," Bromley suggested.

"I can't imagine why she would want to do that, but I have to say it makes more sense than Audrey daring to return here," Poppy concurred.

Bromley called DC Mason and they discussed the possibility of Audrey Wetherby returning to the far north.

"Much more likely Keke Green either committed suicide by the same method or it was a copy-cat murder. It's common knowledge Audrey Wetherby used GHB and oleander to poison her victims. We are looking into the possibility it was a homicide. Tracy says Keke was not suicidal. She was staying with her at the time of her death. Keke just went out for a walk to check on the woman in the cottage down the road and never came back."

"It is a coincidence that the woman in the cottage is now missing," Bromley pointed out.

"She is?" Mason asked. "I didn't know that. Since when?"

"She was driving the same car as the woman from the Air New Zealand flight. She had changed the registration number. Really odd. We are in the process of trying to trace both women."

"This changes things. We need to put a trace on them too. Thanks, Jimmy. I will keep you updated," Mason said.

Jimmy Bromley knew it smelled fishy. Keke Green was poisoned; Anna Ward from the Air New Zealand flight and May Simmons from the cottage in Totara North were both missing.

Audrey Wetherby could be back in the area. Although it was highly unlikely, he needed to get to the bottom of it.

"I'm going out," he called to Poppy.

"Love you," she called back.

# CHAPTER 65

Geoff was a man's man. He had spent his whole life living off the land. A pig hunter, handyman, and pool player. Once a week he would meet up with the boys, drink beer, smoke some pot, and play pool. He had met Mei a couple of years ago. She had hired him to build a cabin. One cabin had turned into seven, and his part-time job had turned into a full-time relationship. Mei had taken on the resort all by herself. She had no one to look after her, not that she needed looking after—she was a strong, independent woman. But she had confided in him she was lonely. Three years ago, she had come to New Zealand to get married and her husband had died, leaving her alone on the remote peninsula. She had purchased the property and business next door belonging to the infamous Audrey Wetherby. Mei said she liked Audrey and didn't believe one word about her being a murderer.

Today, the resort was one of the most prestigious properties in the far north. Visitors came from all over the world. Mei had turned the small business into a multimillion-dollar affair. Now, Covid-19 had changed everything. The borders were closed, and apart from a few frontliners who were staying in six of the cabins, the resort had shut down. Food could not be served, that bar was closed, and there were strict health and safety rules in place for the rented cabins. The usual boat trips out into the bay were forbidden and fishing from the shore was not permitted during Level 4 lockdown.

Geoff was pleased he had over a hundred acres of sea and bush to spend his time in. Most nights, he went out pig hunting; he was after a nasty boar who had been rooting up the paddocks by the waterfall. It was a kiwi zone and no dogs or cats were allowed in the protected areas. He, however, had a couple of pig dogs which he kept locked up. Fuck the rules. They were kiwi-trained and obeyed him and were no threat to the native bird.

He had just returned the dogs to their cages when he thought he saw a woman walking across the ridge toward the tennis courts. It wasn't Mei; she had gone to bed before he went out. *Who the hell is it?* he wondered. By the time he had reached the courts she was gone. He checked out the area and was surprised to see her sitting at a table in the Garden View Restaurant. She was looking out at the bay. When he asked her if he could help her, she spun around and he was face-to-face with a beautiful woman who appeared to be quite at home in her surroundings.

Again, he asked, "Can I help you?"

"Oh dear. I shouldn't be here," she said in such a refined voice. "I was looking for a place to stay and thought the lodge may still be open. I see it isn't. I am so sorry."

"You should be in lockdown. You are not supposed to be changing places." He noticed she stayed sitting at the table as if she was not planning on going anywhere.

"Where have you been staying?" he asked.

"I can't talk about it," she replied. "Let's just say I cannot stay there anymore."

Geoff looked at the lady, who was beginning to shiver in the ocean winds. "Tell you what," he said. "I can put you in one of the cabins tonight and we can discuss your options in the morning with my partner, Mei. Would that work? I must insist you wear a protective mask and gloves when you walk around the property. In the cabin there is antibacterial gel. Please make sure you use it when entering and leaving the cabin at all times. Come with me and I will get you a key."

"Thank you. I really appreciate it. I can pay you for the cabin tomorrow."

"I shouldn't be doing this during lockdown, but no one needs to know. By the way, what is your name?"

"Kathy Lane," she replied.

"Oh, so you are the mysterious Kathy Lane? Name is Geoff. DC Mason said you were looking for Mei. You know her?"

Audrey said, "She may not remember me. It has been a while."

"I am sure she will be pleased to see you. She doesn't have a lot of friends. Always too busy running the resort. How do you two know each other?" he asked, handing her the key to the Kawakawa Chalet.

"I used to know her ex-husband," she said.

"The chalet is the third one down the ridge. You can't miss it. I'll say goodnight then, Kathy. See you in the morning."

"Good night," she replied.

As she stood from the table with poise, her mind was panicked. *Fuck! Fuck! Fuck!*

# CHAPTER 66

Constable Patterson needed to track down the owners of the cottage. He called the Remuera Police again in Auckland and asked them to enter the house and see if they could find any way to get in touch with them. He was concerned when Rose said she had finally contacted their son, who lived in Christchurch, and he said he had not heard from his parents and they had no friends in Hamilton that he knew of. They would have told him if they were staying elsewhere during lockdown. He had not spoken to them for three weeks and was extremely worried. He agreed to have the police enter the house.

When he got word the couple were not in the house and yet their belongings appeared to still be in the residence, he knew something was up. The woman's purse, was inside, as was the man's wallet with his driver's license, credit cards, and a wad of cash. If they were staying with friends, they would have taken their personal belongings.

Their son gave them the license number of their missing car: a 2005 blue Holden Commodore, registration number

AQW115. The police put out an alert to trace it. What the hell was going on?

Patterson called in a forensics team to go over the cottage and see if they could pick up anything that might help them locate Ms. Simmons. She had been gone now for three days. Her friend Anna Ward, who owned the car she was driving, was also missing.

It took another day before the blue Holden was found down a bank a few miles from the Suttons' house. It had been stripped. Nothing much was left of it. Looked like it had been stolen. The couple were still missing.

# CHAPTER 67

Audrey looked around the familiar surroundings. This cabin she knew well. Mei had done a wonderful job turning the old cabin into a luxury chalet. Modern and chic with black-and-white furnishings. The old bathroom and kitchenette were updated and modern. She sat on the bed and kicked off her shoes. Her car was parked down at the bottom of the hill. Did she dare to drive it up here to the resort? *Why bother*, she thought. She was tired and the bed looked so damn inviting. She stripped down to her underwear and climbed under the covers. It had been three years since she had seen Mei. Three years since she'd gotten rid of her husband who treated Mei like shit. Mei had arrived in New Zealand a penniless student wanting to study in a new country. She'd agreed to marry a man twice her age who would pay for her education in return for her hand in marriage. It was a promise he never kept. Audrey had released her of her obligation. Mei inherited the old man's property, and with his life insurance, purchased Tiromoana when Audrey decided to disappear. They had not communicated since.

Would Mei recognize her? This Kathy Lane bore no resemblance to Audrey Wetherby, but she still had misgivings.

It was after ten when Audrey woke to the sound of wood pigeons in the trees eating berries and dropping remnants onto the chalet roof. The waves were crashing against the rocks at the waterfront below. Such familiar sounds that carried memories of her life here. Today would determine her future here in the far north. Would Geoff and Mei allow her to stay? Or would they tell her to leave. There was a basket of personal protection wear on the counter. Wearing her sunglasses, a face mask, and gloves, which she sterilized as instructed, she ventured out to face her hosts. The other cabins and chalets looked vacant. She guessed the frontliners were most likely nurses and doctors and were already at work.

She saw her at the cabana restaurant wiping the tables clean. Mei hadn't changed at all. Petite, young, and attractive. She looked up as Audrey approached.

"You must be Kathy Lane. Geoff said he found you here late last night looking for accommodation. He is such a softie. We are not supposed to open for guests. Did you sleep well?"

Audrey realized Mei had not recognized her. How could she? Her face was mostly covered in protective wear. "I cannot thank you enough," she replied. "I slept like a baby. I am so sorry to intrude."

"Geoff said you knew my ex-husband."

"Oh, that was a long time ago. I used to live around here. I was interested to see what you have done to the property. Amazing! I don't suppose I could stay here while we are in lockdown? I can pay," she added.

Mei thought about it for a moment or two. "I suppose that would be all right. But I cannot offer cleaning services and you have to keep your social distance from any other guests. We are our own bubble here. But as you have just arrived, and we are into week three of shutdown, you must remain in your own bubble."

"I totally understand. I have been in self-isolation since the beginning of lockdown so will remain in my own bubble, no problem. I will go and pick up some supplies and my belongings and return soon."

Audrey couldn't believe her luck. She literally floated all the way down the gravel road to her car. A quick trip into Totara North to pick up her new wardrobe, computer, and personal things and she would return to Tiromoana. She smiled beneath the mask. It was looking to be a good day!

# CHAPTER 68

Poppy was becoming more and more convinced Audrey Wetherby had returned to the far north. She had an ally in Tracy Mason. Having joined forces, the women were phoning residents of Totara North to enquire if they had seen a blonde middle-aged woman in the area. Poppy suggested they get Mei from Tiromoana Resort to join their team.

Tracy wasn't convinced. "She still believes Audrey had nothing to do with the murders," said Tracy.

"How can she deny her DNA was all over the murder scenes?" Poppy was frustrated. "Call her anyway, Audrey may just decide to visit her old killing ground."

"And what about Rose Bright? She sells properties in the area and knows most of the residents," Tracy suggested. "Plus, she is seeing Constable Patterson and may have information we can't get from other sources."

"Great idea. Let's set up a Zoom conference call and start recording our collective knowledge."

Poppy was all business. She had lost her brother. It was a homicide and she was convinced Audrey had something to do with it, but she had never been able to prove it. However, it didn't matter now as Audrey was a suspect in tens of murders that had taken place in the far north. She had disappeared three years ago. Poppy was there. She was staying at Tiromoana at the time of Audrey's disappearance. Her book *The Audrey Murders* was a best-seller. But Jimmy had been devastated when Audrey evaded police. The couple's decision to start a new life in America was one way of putting it all behind them. Coming back had been Poppy's decision. The pandemic meant they may not be able to return home to New Zealand for years. She was pleased Jimmy seemed happy now that he had a new career and something to dig his teeth into again. She had a feeling he wanted to return to the police force.

Tracy called her back to say Mei was on board. She didn't want any trouble at the resort. Her partner, Geoff, was convinced Audrey Wetherby was a serial killer and if she set foot on the property, he wouldn't hesitate to shoot her. Tracy couldn't tell if Mei was being facetious. But Poppy thought Audrey deserved his wrath either way.

They set up a Zoom conference call for ten the following morning. In the meantime, they agreed to collect all the information they could find that may relate to possible murders and connections to the infamous Audrey Wetherby.

Poppy still had her Audrey Wetherby notes from three years ago. She found the old memory stick and downloaded it into a new file called "Audrey Wetherby 2020."

New Zealand were in week three of lockdown. Numbers of new cases were decreasing, with only eight new cases reported, bringing the total number of cases to 1409. The good news was that all eight new cases were linked to existing clusters. It was a positive sign. Jacinda was to announce next Monday when the country would be going into Level 3. Poppy was proud to be a

New Zealander. This was a country that had reacted quickly to Covid-19, putting the country into lockdown early. With a population of just 4.6 million it was a lot easier to trace cases. New Zealand had sixteen clusters. Most of the eleven deaths were from the elderly in rest homes who were frail and had underlying medical conditions.

Poppy wondered where Audrey would be staying. Was she living in Totara North? She hoped the police were doing a door-to-door search of the area. She made a note to ask Rose. She could check with Constable Patterson. Tracy would also know if the Mangonui police station was doing a check in the Hihi area.

Poppy hadn't felt this stimulated in a long time. It was the perfect time, with lockdown still at Level 4. No one was allowed to move residences. If Audrey was in the area, they would find her. She had no doubt about that.

# CHAPTER 69

Mei was having second thoughts about allowing the woman to stay during lockdown. She and Geoff had agreed to only allow frontliners to stay at the resort until the government had reduced the lockdown to Level 2 or below. Even though it looked as though New Zealand would be at Level 3 within the next couple of weeks, Mei was nervous, like the rest of the nation, about contact with other people while the virus was still a risk in the country.

Mei felt a certain amount of guilt being of Asian descent as the virus had originated in her part of the world. She felt people would treat her differently, blame her even. Geoff thought she was being silly, overreacting. He had said, "Asians account for over 15 percent of the New Zealand population now."

When she returned to the house, Geoff was in the shed working on his boat. She told him she had invited the woman to stay in the chalet. She was quick to add the new arrival would pay for the accommodation. Geoff asked if Mei knew why the woman needed a place to stay in the middle of lockdown. Mei said she didn't. She suggested maybe it wasn't safe where she was staying. "The government says we are supposed to report anyone that has to leave their place of residence due to domestic violence or health issues," she said, remembering what had been reported on the news.

"She seems like a nice, respectable lady," Geoff said. "No harm done."

When Mei got a phone call from her friend, Tracy, she was hesitant at first to agree to help her and her friends to track down Audrey. Mei owed her life and her current good fortune to her. Audrey had saved her from her from the horrible man, Steve Sutton, who had come to an arrangement with Mei's family. He promised to pay for her schooling in New Zealand in exchange for her hand in marriage. Mei came from a poor and proud family and when she met the man who was to be her future, she was horrified. He was disgusting, dirty, mean, and violent. Audrey had been there for her. When she offered to sell the resort to her, Mei had no reservations in accepting her offer. When she learned Audrey was responsible for so many murders, she couldn't believe it. However, since meeting Geoff she had changed her mind. Geoff had convinced her Audrey was not who Mei thought she was. Audrey was guilty of murder.

Mei had worked so hard to turn the resort into the success it had become. She didn't want any trouble. Was her life in danger? Would Audrey try and contact her? She hoped not. There was too much at risk.

It had not rained in the far north for months. Just a sprinkling now and then in the past few weeks. But Mei knew a storm was coming. The skies were getting dark. By the time she returned to the house, the heavens had opened. Finally, they were getting rain, and lots of it. The forecast was for heavy rain for the next few days. The water tanks would fill. It was a welcome sight.

# CHAPTER 70

The trip to Totara North was not without its perils. As Audrey entered the Totara North turnoff, she was stopped by a police roadblock. They were checking all IDs and making sure everyone entering the small seaside village had a reason to be there. This was a problem because Kathy only had a California driver's license. She looked in the glove compartment of the old Ute and found a receipt with Matt's name and address in Totara North, which satisfied the needs of the police and permitted her to proceed. They asked her why she was out, and she explained she needed food supplies. She just hoped they didn't ask for proof, which she didn't have. They didn't. By the time she had reached the old villa it was raining heavily. Water was gushing down the driveway and pouring out onto the road below. The harbor waters were rising.

Inside, she began to pack up Kathy's clothes into a suitcase. She was pleased she was leaving the town. She didn't dare return to Hihi, however, until the roadblock was gone. She turned on the television and went to prepare lunch. She was hungry. It was at that moment she realized she was in deep shit. The news announcer had launched into a story. "Audrey Wetherby, the infamous far north serial killer, may have returned to the far north. Tracy Mason, a reporter for the *Northland Newspaper*, thinks she has."

Audrey watched as Tracy appeared on the screen. She recognized her as the woman that had accompanied Keke on the visit to the cottage.

"We suspect Audrey Wetherby has returned to the area. There are a number of disappearances and Keke Green's recent death by GHB and oleander poisoning were Audrey Wetherby's signature weapon of choice."

The reporter asked Tracy if she could provide any more information.

"The police are searching for Anna Ward from the Air New Zealand flight, and May Simmons, who was staying at a cottage in Totara North. Both women have been declared missing and both women were in possession of the same white Nissan car. I personally saw May Simmons at the cottage with Keke just a week ago. Since then, she and her car have gone missing. The owners of the cottage, a middle-aged couple who reside in Auckland, are also missing. We think Audrey Wetherby may have something to do with these disappearances and possibly the murder of my good friend, Keke Green."

"Do you have any proof"? the reporter asked Tracy. "You are married, after all, to Detective Constable Mason at the Mangonui police."

"No, not at this time. But the police have formed a task force to look into the situation," she replied.

Her photo from three years ago was on the screen. "If you see this woman, contact your local police station or call this number," the reporter said. "Do not approach her. She may be dangerous."

Audrey laughed. The photo was old. And as for "dangerous," how hilarious. They made it sound as though she was walking around armed with an AK-47. She was unrecognizable now. Still, she thought, what bad luck this Tracy woman is married to the local detective constable. He must be heading the task force. She wondered if Poppy and Jimmy Bromley had anything to do with this. Audrey didn't doubt for one moment that Poppy would be involved.

# CHAPTER 71

DC Mason was concerned Tracy was in over her head, but she seemed so damn happy and excited about the team she had put together he didn't want to burst her bubble, so to speak. He figured they couldn't do much harm and it was, after all, local news. Audrey Wetherby's murder spree had shocked the quiet rural towns of the far north. And getting the media involved in the search for the missing women may even have positive results.

Five roadblocks had been set up at the junction of the rural towns of Kaeo, Totara North, Taupo Bay, Hihi, and Mangonui. All these towns had only one access road off the main highway, so they were easy to control. The roadblocks would operate from six in the morning to ten at night, making it almost impossible for anyone to avoid being stopped and questioned by police. There were stringent travel rules during lockdown, and no one should be out during the night unless it was an emergency. There were still a couple of roadblocks on the main road heading north. One was at the junction of Mangonui turnoff and other heading north from Kaeo.

Mason was working with all the local stations to coordinate the task force. Constable Patterson had tracked down the car belonging to the owners of the cottage. Whoever took the car didn't leave any trace evidence. A search of the residence also provided no evidence. The whereabouts of the Sutton couple was still unknown.

Jimmy Bromley was assisting the task force with his knowledge of Audrey Wetherby's prior murder cases. His past association with the perpetrator was valuable.

It was a strong team. And their focus was on locating the two missing women, Anna Ward and May Simmons.

Mason's phone buzzed in his pocket. It was Constable Patterson. "We have found the white Nissan," he said. "Plate has been removed, but we are sure it is the same car."

"Where is it?" Mason asked.

"Down the bay road past the Totara North Jetty. Been pushed down an old boat ramp. It's low tide and locals spotted it. We are pulling it out now and looking for a body or bodies. But it looks as though someone didn't want it found."

"Good work, Jimmy. We're finally getting somewhere. Just have to find the two drivers now." Mason hung up the phone.

# CHAPTER 72

M artin was out of intensive care and, thanks to his nursing staff, was finally on the mend. They said he could go home and recuperate there. He didn't know how many days he had spent in hospital, but he just knew he wanted to go home. He had been watching the news and learned his home was in the midst of a media frenzy. May next door had gone missing, his neighbor Keke Green was found dead by the old sawmill, presumed poisoned, and there was a theory the serial killer Audrey Wetherby was back in the neighborhood, resulting in the police setting up a special task force.

His mind went back to the moment he first saw May walking up the pathway to the cottage. Later, when he saw the woman Anna Ward on the television, he had immediately thought they were the same person. He wondered if the police had come to the same conclusion. He would suggest it to Jimmy when he picked him up today to drive him home. Martin had a photographic memory. Once he saw a face, he would remember it. Problem was, he hadn't seen a clear image of either woman. Face masks and scarves prevented facial recognition. He only had a gut instinct to back up his theory. He didn't believe the theory they simply shared the same car. Why would they?

Jimmy told him Poppy had formed her own task force with a local newspaper reporter to track down Audrey Wetherby, whom the reporter, Tracy Mason, believed had killed her good friend, Keke Green.

Why would Audrey Wetherby kill the woman? It seemed a little far-fetched to him. But he was looking forward to sleeping in his own bed again. New cases of the virus were still declining, but they were not out of the woods yet. Martin knew firsthand how bad the virus could be. He'd thought he was going to die.

If May Simmons was Anna Ward and had been on the AIR New Zealand flight that had seven confirmed cases of the virus, then his offer of sharing her bubble was a fucking stupid thing to do. *Serves me right,* he thought. She was a complete stranger. What was he thinking?

If he saw her again, she had some serious explaining to do. On second thought, he never wanted to see her again.

The staff wheeled him out to the patient pick-up area. Jimmy was waiting. "Good to see you, mate," he said as he helped his friend into the car. "You gave us quite a scare."

# CHAPTER 73

The sirens broke the silence. Audrey could see from the window the flashing lights of the police vehicles. They had found the bloody car. She was sure of it. It also meant that they would be preoccupied with pulling the car out of the harbor, which would give her time to head out to Hihi and the resort.

Having already wiped down all surfaces, she turned out the lights and locked the door, taking the keys and one suitcase with her. Getting into the Ute, she headed toward the main highway. She was right: the police had left the roadblock and the road was completely devoid of all traffic. As she approached the Hihi turnoff she waited as a police car with flashing lights headed in the opposite direction. She guessed it was DC Mason on his way to Totara North. She smiled.

When Audrey parked the old Ute outside the chalet, the resort was in darkness. It was late and the rain had not let up. The ground was muddy, and the heavy rain had left deep crevasses in the recently mowed lawn. She made a dive for the front door and noticed the bed was just as she had left it. No cleaning services during lockdown, she remembered, which suited her just fine. She didn't need anyone nosing around in her stuff. Unfortunately, with the rain she didn't dare to start trying to lift heavy concrete paving stones to find her stash. It would make a horrendous mess, not taking into account the fact that she may be seen.

She was taking a huge risk staying at the Tiromoana Resort. But she hoped this would be the last place anyone would look for her. Returning to the scene of many of her crimes gave Audrey a sense of power. No one would find her here. She may even decide to stay. Wouldn't that be ironic.

An hour later, Audrey had filled the cupboards with groceries collected from the villa pantry and placed a dozen chilled bottles of wine in the fridge. The room pleased her. Hanging Kathy's clothes in the wardrobe, she changed for bed. Switching on the television, she listened to the worldwide news. Covid-19 headlined every station. There were 2.2 million cases with almost 155,000 deaths worldwide. New Zealand had another thirteen new cases in the past twenty-four hours. Eradication of the virus seemed a while off yet. She, like the rest of the country, was trapped with borders closed. The situation was the same in most countries around the world. Who would have guessed she would be lying in bed in Tiromoana? She turned out the light and was asleep before the television sleep timer had turned off.

# CHAPTER 74

DC Mason's conversation with Martin had him thinking. Were Anna Ward and May Simmons the same person? There was a strong possibility. They had not been able to find any information on either woman. From the moment Anna Ward purchased the white Nissan, she had simply disappeared. And as she disappeared, May Simmons appeared at the cottage in Totara North in the same car. At the same time, the couple who owned the cottage disappeared. Now the car had surfaced in the waters off Totara North headlands. But he could not link the case to Keke Green's death.

DC Mason had arranged to do Covid-19 testing with the two hundred residents of Totara North starting tomorrow morning. The government had already done a thousand random tests at supermarkets throughout the country and, to date, not one person tested positive for the virus. Experts said there would need to be tens of thousands of tests before the information could be relied upon. He figured adding another two hundred tests would not cause unnecessary hardship within the current testing program.

Besides, it may also give Jimmy and the tracing division the information they need to know how Martin had contracted the virus.

When he arrived home, he heard Tracy holding a Zoom conference with her sleuth group. They were discussing May Simmons.

Tracy was holding court. "Surely someone will recognize her in the area. I only got a glimpse of her through the glass door, and she was hiding her face with a scarf, but I got a good look at her. If I saw her again, I would recognize her. She was thin, almost too thin, dark hair, slight American accent. Expensive clothes."

"Completely different description to the Audrey Wetherby I got to know," Poppy said. "She was rather loud and spoke with a slightly English accent, more Christchurch girls' school. She was certainly not thin and was big-breasted. Always had blonde hair pulled up into a bob on the top of her head or worn down in a pageboy hairstyle. She did not have particularly expensive taste in clothes. No flair at all."

"But May Simmons is similar to Anna Ward," Rose said. "The woman you describe sounds like the way they described Anna Ward."

"Do you think they are the one and the same?" Mei asked. "Sorry I was late, just had a few chores to do at the resort."

"Hi, Mei." The group welcomed her.

"That is what I am beginning to think," Tracy said. "If so, she can't get very far during lockdown. The police are doing a door-to-door search in Totara North. They will find her soon enough."

"You don't suppose she was in her car when it went into the harbor?" Rose asked.

"They didn't find her, and the car was close to the shore. If she was going to kill herself, she wouldn't have removed the registration plates," Poppy said.

DC Mason listened to the women and then went and poured himself a drink. His wife was having so much fun he didn't want to disturb her. They had made some good points. He was beginning to believe he was dealing with only one woman, and she must have had something to hide or why would she destroy the car?

She wouldn't get far. They would have Totara North closed down tomorrow while they did the search. Mason was sure of one thing: If she was there, they would find her.

# CHAPTER 75

Audrey's plan was to spend the day in her cozy little chalet listening to the occasional shower on the roof. The pressure was off. Lockdown meant that no one would be knocking at her door or checking on her. She was in her own happy bubble wearing a pair of Kathy's designer pajamas. But her peace of mind was soon shattered as she heard a knock on her door.

Audrey opened the curtain to see two health workers fully covered in PPE standing at the front door of chalet. *Fuck!* She swore inwardly. They had seen her.

"Hi, we are staying in the chalets here at Tiromoana. I'm Mary, this is Brian. We are just heading off to test all the residents in Totara North for Covid-19. Geoff and Mei said you were staying here. Kathy Lane, isn't it? Just wanted to stop by and say hi and see if there is anything you need."

Audrey suspected she had brought the virus with her from the USA. Her dry cough and lack of sense of smell and taste were two key symptoms of the virus. However, that had been over three weeks ago.

Audrey opened the window to talk to them. Keeping the required distance, she said, "Hello, nice to meet you both. You guys are amazing. I don't need anything, but thank you. Take care."

"Will do," they said.

*Shit!. This is not good.* The health workers knew her name. Surely Kathy and Matt Lane would be on the list of residents in Totara North. They would expect her to be in the villa, not here. Questions would be asked why she was staying fifteen minutes away in Hihi. There was no logical answer. She would have to find her cash and get out of here, now. It had stopped raining. Where were Mei and Geoff? If they were at the house over on the far ridge, she would have time to search for her money.

Audrey changed into jeans and a sweatshirt and went in search of a spade. Outside, there was no sign of the owners. She would work as fast as she could. She had figured out where the old shed was in relation to the restaurant. She was wrong when she had thought the money was buried under the paving stones. After pacing out the area she now knew the old shed area was a garden planted in succulents and bromeliads. It was a relief. Alone on the resort grounds, she found a spade in a garden shed.

Digging was a slow process. Each time she dug an area and was unsuccessful, she would replant it. She repeated this process until her spade hit a solid object. She had found it! She checked she was still alone and removed the familiar metal box. It was rusty and dirty. She brushed off the surface dirt and opened the box. The black trash bag was still inside. Quickly she closed the lid and finished replacing the plants. Using a nearby hose, she cleaned the area. A quick glance at the garden and you could not tell it had been disturbed. Audrey prided herself on her gardening skills.

Once inside her chalet, she laid the box on a towel on the floor. Before she could open it, there was a knock at her door.

"Kathy, it is Mei. I am just going to put an invoice under the door. The chalet is $100 per night so I have made the invoice out for one week. You can just pay online. Is that okay?"

"Yes, that's great. No problem. I will put the money into your account today."

"Great. Stay safe."

Had Mei seen her? Surely not. She would have said something. But the timing was way too close for comfort. She was beginning to feel uneasy.

Finally, Audrey had her money. She pried open the box and tore at the bag. It was stuffed with shredded newspaper. Furious, she searched for her money. All she found was a note.

*Audrey, if you are reading this, you have returned for your money.*
*We found it when we removed the cottage.*
*Geoff and I needed the money to finish the resort.*
*We know you will understand.*

# CHAPTER 76

The door-to-door testing was a long process. Almost half of the properties were vacant. They were holiday homes and citizens had been advised to stay at home and not go to their holiday houses during lockdown. It still required a personal visit to each property. Today they had tested over seventy residents. Tomorrow they would get the results.

DC Mason remembered Constable Patterson's request to check on the Tiromoana Resort in Hihi. He didn't see the need to check on it again. Mai and Geoff seemed happy in their bubble. The resort was closed to the public and only a few front-liners were staying in the cabins. Each in their own bubble.

When his phone rang, he was surprised to hear from the Remuera branch. "Senior Constable Briggs here. I understand you are looking for the missing couple in our area that disappeared three weeks ago. They have been found in a recycling dumpster in Manukau City. No one has been working in the center during lockdown. Today a couple walking their dog found the bodies. They have been initially identified as Bruce and Mary Sutton. These names were on a document in the old man's pocket. I understand you had put out an APB on them."

"Yes, I did," Mason replied. "Have you established their cause of death?"

"Homicide for sure. They wouldn't have been hanging around that neighborhood by their own choice. A well-to-do couple from Remuera had no business in Manukau. There are no signs of injury. We're running a toxicology report, and checking for any DNA at the scene."

"Excellent. Thank you. Keep me informed, especially regarding the DNA and result of the toxicology report. The couple have a son in Christchurch. Have you contacted him yet?" Mason asked.

"Yes, he is coming up to confirm their identity. Should be here tomorrow morning. We are pretty sure it's the couple but it's difficult to identity from the remains. They have been in the bin for at least three weeks, the coroner suspects."

"Do you have any leads as to whom may be responsible for their deaths?" Mason asked.

"Not yet. The neighbors saw a middle-aged, thick-set blonde woman visit them about the time they went missing. But we don't have any further information. They said they did see the couple in their car the next day but someone else was driving, they couldn't see who. They presumed someone was taking them to get groceries. A neighbor, maybe. It's not unusual for neighbors to take elderly couples out for some fresh air and to do their shopping. We are checking around the neighborhood. Will keep you informed."

"Middle-aged, thick-set blonde woman, you said. Any more description on the woman?"

"Nope, that's all we got," Constable Briggs said.

"Thanks for your call. Appreciate it. We will let you know if we can add anything from our end that may help the investigation," Mason said.

When he hung up, he was more convinced than ever that his wife and her group may be on to something. *If that description doesn't fit Audrey Wetherby, I will eat my hat! If they find her DNA, we have her.*

# CHAPTER 77

Tracy's sleuth group was buzzing with the news. The women had created a virtual photo board of everyone of interest in the case. Looking at the photos of Audrey, Anna, and May, the group found it difficult to tie Audrey into the mix. Anna and May could easily be the same person. Their faces had been disguised by scarves, hats, and sunglasses. Audrey, on the other hand, just didn't fit the description.

"Tomorrow I will use Photoshop and change Audrey's appearance as we used to know her to what she may look like today if she dyed her hair black and lost a lot of weight. She could have had a facelift or a nose job," Tracy said. "If she is the same person, that would explain a lot."

"Are you sure you have not seen any of these women, Mei?" Poppy asked.

"No. I would recognize Audrey if I saw her again. As for the other two women, Anna and May, I have not. We are closed for lockdown. We only have a few medical staff staying in the cabins.

Oh." she paused. "I did allow another woman to stay in one of the chalets. Her name is Kathy Late. Nice woman."

"Holy shit! What does she look like?" Poppy asked.

"I didn't really get to see her face; she was wearing sunglasses and a face mask."

"What was her voice like? Was it Audrey?"

"It was three years ago when I met Audrey. I didn't really know her well. She was very supportive, wasn't she, Poppy? You were there. Audrey was wonderful. I still find it difficult to think she would ever hurt anyone. Geoff thinks I'm crazy. This woman has a soft-spoken voice; she is quite young. Oh, you can ask Steve, Tracy. He met her at the Hihi roadblock a couple of days ago."

"Kathy Lane." Tracy repeated the name. "I will ask him. Same time tomorrow, ladies. Let's sign off."

When Tracy asked her husband if he remembered a Kathy Lane staying at the Tiromoana Resort, he was surprised. "She's staying there?" he asked. "I thought they didn't know who she was."

"Well, apparently they do. She is staying there now, anyway. Who is Kathy Lane?" she asked.

"She said she was a friend of Mei's. I stopped her going into Hihi the other day. Driving an old Ute. Dressed to kill."

"Where was she from? Do you know?"

"She didn't have her license on her, if I remember correctly, but she had some ID with an address in Totara North. I checked her registration. It was legitimate; it belonged to a Matt Lane. I guessed it was her husband. It didn't look like the sort of car she would be driving."

"You don't suppose it's the same woman we are searching for?" Tracy asked.

"You have a vivid imagination, Trace," he teased.

# CHAPTER 78

There was no need to stay at the resort. Her money was gone and spent. She would return to the villa and take her chances. Hopefully they had finished their testing.

It was too risky to leave at night. She would wait until tomorrow morning. Audrey looked at the invoice left by Mei. She put on protective gloves and wrote her a note:

*Hi Mei, thanks for the use of the chalet.*
*I have left $200, hope that covers my stay.*
*I just needed a break away from a personal situation.*
*I really appreciate your kindness.*
*Stay Safe,*
*Kathy*

Friendly, non-committal, and cheerful. Everything Audrey was not feeling. Mei would have to pay for her betrayal. She would regret crossing her. Audrey would retrieve what Mei owed her by some other means. But tonight was not the night.

The morning light came too soon. Audrey's cash flow needed to be infused and she had come up with a plan to do just that.

She removed her clothes from the wardrobe and packed them into her suitcase. She returned all the groceries and wine into a cardboard box and packed them away in the trunk of her car along with the old tin box. She inspected the chalet. She had worn gloves and had wiped down all the surfaces. This was not a time to be leaving her DNA or fingerprints anywhere. Leaving the note, the keys, and the cash on the table, she quietly departed Tiromoana and returned to Kathy's villa.

The roadblocks were gone. The police tape around the old sawmill had been removed. There were no signs of health workers. The main street was deserted. Even where she had dumped the car was dark and desolate. It was as though the town had returned to lockdown normality.

The house was just as she had left it. She returned the groceries to the pantry, the wine to the fridge, the clothes to the wardrobe, and sat on the bed. *I guess this is home,* she thought. Opening her laptop, she checked the morning news.

*The bodies of an elderly couple were found yesterday in a dumpster in Manukau. The police expect their identities to be announced later today. They are treating their deaths as homicide. The couple had been missing from their Remuera home for four weeks.*

Audrey sighed. *They've found them. Just as well I moved out of their bloody cottage. I can't believe they found them in the dumpster! I drove them to the other side of the damn city to dispose of them when I could have just left them in their bloody car a few miles from their house. Well, that was a fucking waste of time.* Audrey knew there was no way they could link the Suttons' murders to her. She checked the rest of the news. Numbers of new Covid-19 cases were dropping daily. Only nine new cases today. Tomorrow Jacinda would announce when the country would go into Level 3. It would be four weeks in a few days since they went into Level-4 shutdown. There was a fear that if they relaxed the restrictions too early, the virus could take hold again.

There was no new news about Keke's death or the car in the harbor. It was old news now. Covid-19 still controlled every news channel and newspaper. It seemed to be the only news anyone wanted to hear. She felt confident that she could live her life now as Kathy Lane. It was sad how her father had passed away during lockdown as no funeral could be held. She may have to sell the house when the borders open so she can return to California. While in lockdown she would find out who was Matt's lawyer and produce a death certificate. She presumed Kathy was the beneficiary of his will. It would be a simple process to put the house on the market. It must be worth over five hundred thousand. It would help pay back some of the money Mei stole from her. The thought of Mei was not a pleasant one.

Before she could feel safe back in Totara North, she had one task to perform. There was one person in town who could recognize her as May. She had not seen him in weeks. His curtains had been shut the last couple of times she had passed his house.

It had been simple lust that had caused her to make this mistake. She had let her guard down. She would have to fix it.

# Chapter 79

Mei was surprised to find her new guest had already left. Kathy Lane had left the chalet spotlessly clean and paid cash for her stay. Mei pocketed the cash and returned to the house. Geoff had gone fishing off their private beach. She walked down to join him.

"She's gone. Paid cash and just left," she told him.

"She was a strange one. Gave me the spooks. Glad she's gone."

"You know, Tracy thinks she may be tied up with the women who have gone missing in Totara North," Mei mentioned.

"You women and your detective group," scoffed Geoff.

"Still, I wish I got a better look at her. Did you get a good look at her?"

"It was dark, and she was wearing a hoodie, but I did see her face. She was quite a stunning woman. But, as I said, it was dark. I doubt I would recognize her if I saw her again. I am not good with faces, you know that," Geoff said.

"Oh well. Are you allowed to be fishing during lockdown? I thought it was not allowed."

Geoff was winding in his line. "Got one!" he said. "It is our bloody property; we can do what we want."

Mei smiled. She had really fallen in love with this guy. He was older than her and made her feel safe and protected. She left him at the beach and returned to the house. She had a Zoom conference coming up soon with the girls. She felt bad she didn't have more information on Kathy Lane. She was enjoying their sleuth group, as they called it.

When she reported Kathy Lane had disappeared, Tracy said they knew who she was. Kathy Lane lived down by the jetty in Totara North. Her husband was going to visit her tomorrow. The girls couldn't wait to hear what she had to say. Why had she stayed at the resort in Hihi? Did she look like the missing women? It was exciting.

"I hear they have confirmed the elderly couple, found murdered in Manukau, are Bruce and Mary Sutton. I wonder if the elusive May Simmons has heard the news?" Poppy said, then continued. "And poor Martin, thank God he is feeling so much better. He almost died. He thinks it was May who gave him the virus. The good news is he can identify her. He is the only person that actually has seen her face-to-face in broad daylight. He spent over an hour drinking wine and talking with her."

"Holy shit! He actually was on a date with her?" Rose was shocked. "Does he think she is Anna Ward from the flight?"

"Apparently he said he thought they may be the same person. He told Jimmy she looked very familiar to Anna Ward, but he couldn't say for sure. Martin will work with the police to create a sketch of May Simmons so the police have a better description of her," Poppy said.

Mei was impressed. She felt a sense of belonging for the first time since she had arrived in New Zealand. She really had no girlfriends. Who would have believed it would be Audrey Wetherby that would give her this special gift?

# Chapter 80

It was midnight. Martin had slept most of the day. The virus had made him feel so incredibly tired. Although his breathing had improved considerably, he still had a cough and his body ached. He was restless. Tomorrow they would hear if the country would be out of Level 4. Not that it made any difference to him. He would be isolated for some time yet. He didn't think too many people would want to visit a Covid-19 patient.

He was wrong. He heard a faint tap at his front door. *Who the fuck can it be at mid-night?* he wondered. He guessed it must be the police or a health worker checking on him. He grabbed a robe, turned on the hall light, and opened the door.

She was dripping wet. She looked forlorn and pathetic standing outside in the pouring rain. "Can I come in?" she asked. "I need to tell you something."

"What? That you gave me Covid-19 and you're sorry?"

"You have the virus?!" she said. "I had no idea. I've been away. Are you okay? Are you contagious?"

"I guess you can come in. After all, you can't catch it twice, they say."

Martin opened the door and she came in, standing dripping in the hallway. "Let me get you a towel."

When he returned, she had taken off her coat and shoes. He wrapped the towel around her shoulders. She took the towel and rubbed her hair. She was wearing a pair of his gloves.

"You have cut your hair," he said.

"Thanks for letting me in. Were you serious? Did you get Covid-19?" she asked. "You know, when I arrived here, I had a dry cough, but after a couple of days in bed I was fine. I had wondered if I'd caught the virus. But what makes you think I gave it to you?"

"You were the only person I had been close to in weeks. It had to be you."

"Oh, Martin, I am so sorry. How can I make it up to you?"

Martin looked at the beautiful woman, wet, vulnerable, and bloody sexy, and said, "Would you like a drink?"

"I would love one. Are you sure you're up to it? You look pretty bad," she said.

"Thanks for the compliment. You look pretty good to me."

She laughed. He poured them both a drink. "Do you mind if I at least wash my face and clean my teeth?" he said. "I've been in bed all day."

"Go ahead. No hurry," she replied with a smile.

# CHAPTER 81

Audrey knew what she needed to do. She took the risk Martin would open the door to her in the middle of the night. She walked from the villa, keeping to the shadows so as not to be seen by any nosy neighbors. When he opened the door, he looked terrible. When he mentioned Covid-19, she knew she really had no choice.

They sat and drank wine while Martin filled her in on what had been going on. "The police and the government health tracing people have been looking for you. They found your car in the harbor and traced it back to an Anna Ward who arrived off the Air New Zealand flight with the infected passengers. When I was diagnosed with it, they figured it must have come from you."

"I had no idea. That is awful. Anna and I were on the same flight from California. She loaned me her car and I was going to return it to her but she said to dump it as she had seen it on the television and she didn't want to be dragged into the whole Covid-19 scene."

"And your friends who own the cottage have just been found dead, murdered," Martin said.

Audrey reached over and felt his forehead. "You still have a temperature," she said. "Why don't you lie down. I can sit with you for a while. You don't look well at all."

"I don't feel well at all," he said.

Audrey helped him into bed. She went into the bathroom and dampened a flannel and placed it on his forehead. "You should have let me know. I would have been here for you."

"I rang for an ambulance and was intensive care for days. I have just returned home," he explained.

"I think you should have stayed there."

Audrey watched as his breathing became more restricted. Before long, Martin was dead.

She sat on the side of his bed watching the man. She would have had sex with him if he had asked. He hadn't.

Any sign of a visitor was removed. The glasses were returned to the cabinet, wine returned to the fridge, the entrance hall wiped dry using the towel he had used to dry her hair. She took one look around his bungalow. It was pristine. She put the towel in her bag and closed the door behind her. She left it unlocked as he had done.

Audrey knew now she had to provide the police with proof that Anna Ward and May Simmons were the same person and responsible for the recent murders. It was the only way to get them off her back.

The cottage was in darkness. The rain had not stopped. It was a blessing for the farmers and would provide much-needed water for the far north. It would not take long to establish solid proof that May Simmons was a fake and had murdered the Suttons and Keke Green. Her clothes were still in the closet along with a number of her hats. All had been washed and hung carefully using gloves to avoid leaving any DNA on them. She chose a handbag and inside it placed Anna Ward and May Audrey

Simmons's passports, driver's licenses, bank cards, and the sale and purchase agreement for the cottage in Totara North. There was no makeup as it would contain DNA. She did leave a new lip gloss that she carefully opened and placed in the bag, and a burner phone with no sim card.

She had already removed any food she had partly consumed and dug a hole in the garden to dispose of it.

Looking around the cottage, she was sure she had created a scene that would be credible to the police. A scene that would prove Anna Ward, aka May Simmons, was solely responsible for the murders and the case would be closed.

She just had one more finishing touch: the suicide note.

*To Whom It May Concern:*
*My name is Anna Ward and I am solely responsible for the deaths of Bruce and Mary Sutton. Things got out of hand when I tried to purchase the cottage and I am sorry.*
*I used a combination of GHB and oleander oil, which I have used before to poison rodents. It has been my poison of choice as it does not cause any pain.*
*When Keke Green began to suspect that I might be involved in their disappearance, I panicked and used the poison on her too.*
*Anna Ward and May Simmons are one and the same person. I have been living as May Simmons since arriving in Totara North.*
*I dumped the car in the harbor when I saw the police were searching for it.*
*When I arrived in New Zealand, I suspected I had Covid-19.*
*I have decided to take my own life. I cannot live with the fear of spending the rest of my life in jail. You will not find my body. I am a good swimmer and will take GHB and swim out in the sea as far as I can make it before the drug takes effect.*
*Anna Ward, aka May Simmons*

Audrey placed a vial of GHB and oleander oil next to the note on the kitchen table and left the cottage.

# CHAPTER 82

Jimmy Bromley was feeling guilty he had not been to visit his friend Martin since he had dropped him off at home from the hospital a couple of days ago. They had been so busy trying to get information to the government in order for the prime minister and the whole Covid-19 team to make the decision at four o'clock this afternoon as to when the country would be going out of Alert Level 4 into Alert Level 3. Level 3 is still classified as a high risk as the disease is not contained. People would still be required to stay at home in their bubble. Physical distancing still applied; people must stay in their household bubbles but can expand to reconnect with close family or care-givers. Schools 1–10 years and early childhood education could reopen but children should learn at home if possible. People must work from home unless not possible. Business can open premises but cannot physically interact with customers. It is a new world, Bromley reflected. New Zealand, like the rest of the planet, is living in a Covid-19 world.

Knowing he couldn't leave his office, he called DC Mason and asked if he could check on Martin if he was heading out that way. He presumed the health workers would be following up with him. But he was concerned. He had tried to call him a number of times with no luck. Although he imagined Martin would be sleeping most of the day, it still left him feeling uneasy.

It was almost noon when they told him DC Mason was on the phone and it was urgent. He excused himself from the meeting, explaining he had to take the call, and asked the operator to put it through to his office.

"I have bad news, Jimmy. Your friend Martin has passed away. Looks like the virus got him. I am so sorry. We have notified the Department of Health, who are handling the situation. I will keep you updated."

Bromley was shocked. "He shouldn't have left the hospital. I thought it was too early. Thanks for letting me know. Appreciate it."

Returning to the meeting, Bromley explained to the group that the virus had just taken one of his best friends. It was proof they couldn't be too careful. It was going to be a difficult decision as to when to lower the alert level. People were still getting infected and deaths were still happening.

Experts advised if New Zealand were to stay at Level 4 long enough, there would be a chance the country could do what no other country could do: eliminate the virus. However, the debate was whether to protect the health of New Zealanders by staying in Level 4 or go to Level 3 to help the economy. The Reserve Bank had calculated that for every month the country stays in alert Level 4, the GDP reduces by 35 percent for that month. A tough dilemma.

In only four hours, the decision would be announced. Bromley and the others had some tough choices to make.

As soon as the meeting was over, he called Poppy. She was devastated. "Poor Martin."

# CHAPTER 83

T he country was waiting with anticipation for the prime minister's announcement. The decision would affect the lives of all New Zealanders. Some could finally go back to work. Constable Patterson was no different from any other New Zealander; he knew the decision would affect his new girlfriend, Rose. It made him smile to think he was thinking of her as his girlfriend. Rose had property owners and purchasers who had been adversely impacted by the lockdown. Now they could hire moving trucks, valuers, complete settlements. She was anxious to get back to work.

He had taken a drive to Totara North to check on the cottage for Rose. She was concerned the property was not secure since May Simmons had gone missing and her car had been found in the harbor. As he pulled into the driveway, he saw an ambulance at the neighbor's. Health workers wearing PPE were placing someone in the vehicle. He stopped to enquire and was shocked to learn that the man in the house had just died of the virus.

He continued up the driveway to the cottage and knocked at the door. No answer. He had Rose's permission to enter the cottage, and he found it vacant. No sign that anyone had been there recently. On the kitchen table he saw a note and a small vial. He radioed in to the station. "We have a situation here. I am at the cottage in Totara North. I need forensics, ASAP."

His phone rang, it was Rose. "It's not good," he told her. " There is no one here, but there is a note. I cannot go into the details, but the cottage is fine. It will be closed off for a few days while forensics check it out."

"What happened? Can't you tell me?" she asked.

"There is a suicide note. That is all I can say. See you tonight."

# CHAPTER 84

After hearing the news, Rose called an urgent Zoom conference. The revelation that there was a suicide note left at the cottage was paramount.

"Who has died? Anna Ward? May Simmons? Audrey Wetherby? All three in one?" Tracy asked Rose. "Did Andy say?"

"He couldn't tell me more. Just that there was a suicide note."

"Maybe Steve has heard. I will call him. This is big news. I need to write the story for the afternoon edition of the paper," Tracy said.

Poppy was quiet. "I just heard our good friend Martin Melrose died of Covid-19 this morning. He had just been released from hospital. He lived next door to the cottage."

"That is awful, I am so sorry. What is happening to the world?" Mei said.

And today, of all days. Everyone was waiting to hear when the country would go to Alert Level 3. The suicide of a woman in Totara North was not likely to hit the front pages.

Still, Tracy needed to get to the bottom of it. She called Steve, who had heard on the radio that forensics were at the scene. He was heading over there. If only she could have a copy of the note. She asked Steve if the police would release the note to the press. He said he would find out and let her know.

She couldn't write the article without all the facts. It was so damn frustrating. She decided, as a reporter, she should be able to interview the police at the property. She changed into full personal protection gear and headed out to Totara North. If there was a story, she would be the first to write about it.

The cottage was buzzing with activity when she arrived. She saw Steve and Andy there. She realized she was completely unrecognizable in her gear. She looked like one of the forensic team. She walked into the kitchen and the note was still lying on the table next to a vial of liquid. She took a quick picture of them both while everyone was busy. She didn't dare stay a minute longer and returned to her car. She couldn't believe she got away with it. As soon as she reached the Totara North turnoff she pulled over and looked at the photo. "Holy shit!" she said aloud. She knew she had hit the jackpot. She couldn't wait to get home and write the article. It would be online in just a couple of hours.

# CHAPTER 85

Audrey watched the four o'clock press conference with Jacinda Ardern. She imagined the rest of New Zealand was doing the same. The popular prime minister announced New Zealand would be in one more week of lockdown and move to Alert Level 3 at 11:59 p.m. on Monday, April 27. Nine new cases were reported today, all linked to existing clusters, for a total of 1,440 cases with 974 recovered. Overall, there had been 86,305 tests done, which put New Zealand amongst the highest in the world in testing per capita. Jacinda said she didn't want to risk all the work done to date for just two working days, referring to the Anzac holiday weekend. It was an expected decision. More emphasis would be put on community testing amongst medical staff and essential businesses.

From the villa Audrey could not see any activity on the main road. She had heard an ambulance a few hours ago and wondered if Martin had been found dead in his bed. She wondered how long it would be before the cottage was searched. Since the bodies of the owners had been identified, she imagined the police would search the property. She knew once the police read the note, the heat would be off.

Audrey had understood returning to New Zealand was not going to be easy. But she had not predicted just how complicated her life would become. Her vision of living in the little cottage overlooking the harbor was not to be. Reclaiming her money was now impossible. The need to cover her tracks almost daily had become tiresome. She looked around the old villa. It was not her choice of accommodation. It was too big and needed repair; the gardens were overgrown and the access difficult. In order to put it on the market it would need to be renovated. She had access to Kathy and Matt's bank accounts, but even then, she would be scratching to finance the project.

As a lawyer now, she could easily access legal documents. Matt's will was simple: it all went to her. He had a small life insurance policy which she would claim once she created his death certificate. No one would be interested in how he had been buried. Lockdown prevented funerals of more than one person. They would have expected her to attend the service alone with no fuss.

Audrey put an ad on the local community Facebook page for a builder. The sooner she could start on the house renovations, the sooner she could put it on the market. She was surprised to get an immediate response. A man left his name and phone number and said to call. She did. He said he lived locally and could start right away. As long as they kept social distancing, he didn't think it a problem. He could come by tomorrow and see what needs to be done and give her a quote. She agreed.

She felt it was a fresh start. She liked being the lawyer, Kathy Lane. She had a new wardrobe she was really enjoying, a new hairstyle, a home to call her own, and a new project of turning the old villa into a valuable asset. Life was looking up.

# CHAPTER 86

Johnny Woods was listening to the press conference on Covid-19. Another week in lockdown didn't really make much difference to him. He worked when he wanted to. He did miss going out on the boat. He would go down to the jetty in the early morning and drop a line over. No one seemed to care. His whole life was adhering to social distancing—he wasn't much for socializing. Johnny considered himself fit, healthy, and a bit of a loner. He was in his late forties, never married, never wanted to be. Most women around Totara North were rural, country folk. Mostly retired. Johnny liked to look good. He wore Levi's jeans and cotton shirts.

He checked his Facebook account and saw a post from a lady looking for a builder. He wouldn't mind some extra money and it was local. She said she lived in Totara North. When she called, he thought she sounded refined and rather sexy. Not the usual local type. He was looking forward to meeting her tomorrow. He went down into his workspace to check his tools and equipment. He was well stocked. Had purchased a lot of supplies before lockdown. He thought he might do some work around his property, but that didn't happen. He couldn't even think what he had done in the past four weeks. Nothing much. Time to do some physical work.

He opened a beer and started sorting out his tools. He would load his truck tomorrow. Maybe he'd be able to start straight-away. Kathy Lane, she said her name was. He wondered if she was old Matt Lane's daughter.

# CHAPTER 87

Tracy read over the article for the third time. She didn't want to get her husband into any trouble, as the police may think he'd given her the information. For that reason she had decided it would be too risky to print the suicide letter. Instead, she gave reference to it.

MURDERS IN LOCKDOWN — SOLVED?
*This afternoon, the police did a check on a property in Totara North owned by Bruce and Mary Sutton, whose recent deaths are being treated as homicide. Since lockdown, the property had been occupied by a woman, May Simmons, who claimed to be a friend of the Suttons. However, May Simmons was recently connected to the missing woman Anna Ward from the Air New Zealand flight which had seven confirmed cases of Covid-19. The Department of Health have been attempting to track Anna Ward's movements to no avail. However, a suicide note has been found at the Totara North premises which indicates that May Simmons and Ann Ward are one and the*

*same and the woman is claiming to be responsible for both the Suttons' murder and the recent murder of Totara North resident Keke Green. May Simmons's car was found ditched in the Whangaroa harbor a few days ago. The police do not know the whereabouts of Ms. Simmons at this time. A search for her body is underway.*

Tracy wondered if she should pass it by her husband before filing it and decided not to.

She sent the article to all of the national media outlets. She knew it would make the evening news. She also sent it to all local media in the far north.

Then, she called her sleuth group to fill them in.

# CHAPTER 88

"How the fuck did you get that information?" DC
Mason was really pissed. "Who gave it to you? Did
Andy tell Rose Bright? Did she tell you?"

Mason was furious with Tracy. The article she'd written
made him look bad. Thank goodness it hadn't made the main
news, despite her efforts. Jacinda Ardern's announcement that
the country would get to Alert Level 3 next Tuesday was the
story of the day. Tracy's story hardly got a mention. *Thank goodness,* he thought. The local news media gave it more press, but it
was pretty much a non-event in the big picture of things. No one
cared about an old couple's demise or a woman who may or may
not have committed suicide.

"Why didn't you wait until we were ready to get the media
involved?" Mason asked.

"I wanted to get it out first," she said meekly. "I thought it
would be a big story. Seems the whole country is more interested
in Covid-19. A couple of months ago, this would have been the
top story of the day."

Mason fumed in silence.

"Who is looking for the body?" Tracy dared to ask.

"The coastguards are out in the harbor, but she could be anywhere. She could still be alive. The suicide note may be just to put us off her trail. We are looking at all angles," Mason said.

"You think she could still be alive?" The look on Tracy's face was pure confusion. Realization dawning on her, she hung her head and her shoulders sagged. "You're right, sweetheart. I was so excited to get a story, I wasn't thinking. Do you want to know how I got the information?" She showed him her phone. "I took the photo in the cottage. I was there. I dressed in PPE gear and no one even realized I wasn't supposed to be there."

"Shit! Trace, what were you thinking?"

"I know. Now you have me worried. She could still be out there. I feel like a fool," Tracy admitted.

Mason looked at his wife. She looked so pitiful. How could he stay mad at her? He loved her. Her crazy ways, her impulsiveness, it was what attracted him to her in the first place. He put his arms around her. "Come here, Trace. You are forgiven," he said. "But please don't do that again. You might have actually done some good. If she is alive, she will think we have gone along with her story and closed the case. And that is not going to happen until we find her body."

# CHAPTER 89

Audrey found herself singing. She felt great. A huge weight had been lifted from her shoulders. She read Tracy Mason's article online. The police would spend days searching the harbor, find nothing, and then eventually give up. She would be free!

She heard a truck coming up the steep driveway and looked out the window. A tall, good-looking man was walking up the pathway to her back door.

"Johnny Woods," he said as she opened the door. "And you must be Kathy Lane. I know your old dad."

Audrey took one look at the man standing in front of her and fell instantly in lust. He was gorgeous. Strong, lean, and looked so damn good in his jeans. He reminded her of a carpenter stripper you see in those silly GIFs, only this GIF was walking into her house. If she was lucky, he would be walking into her house every day for many weeks. She had no doubt he was right for the job.

"My dad unfortunately passed away recently," she said. "Please do come in and I can show you what needs fixing. Well, actually, most of this old villa needs restoring I want to get it looking great to put it on the market. Maybe you can have a look around and tell me what you think."

She noticed he took off his boots inside the door. Nice boots. Nice butt. He even smelled good as he walked past her. Not bottled scent but a natural musky odor. He did not appear to be particularly interested in her, which made him even more desirable. After she had taken him through the villa pointing out areas that were in need of repair, she said, "I will meet you back in the kitchen. I'm just making myself a coffee, would you like one too?"

"That would be great," he said. "I'll just go outside and check the roof, windows, exterior boards, and the decking."

She brewed the coffee and found some cheese and crackers and waited for him to join her. She felt like a schoolgirl. Her heart was beating hard in her chest. She watched him out the window. He had found a ladder and was climbing onto the roof. She turned on some music, light and unobtrusive. She checked her makeup and undid her top button of her blouse. She was wearing Kathy's tight capri rust-colored pants and a white cotton blouse. She was aware he had adhered to the rule of six feet apart for the social distancing requirements during the tour of the house. He was not wearing gloves or a mask, however. She figured if she did have Covid-19 four weeks ago she would be immune by now and not contagious.

He joined her at the table. He told her that yes, he could do the job; it would take at least three weeks, maybe longer, and he charges forty dollars per hour. He had brought his tools with him if she wanted him to start right away. He asked for pen and paper and started to write out a list of what he felt needed repairing. He couldn't get building supplies until next Tuesday when they were at Level 3.

Audrey couldn't believe her luck. He was a gift from heaven. She agreed to his terms and reviewed the list of repairs. She told him he could leave his tools in the workspace under the house. It had a large workbench and she would provide him with a key, so he had access at all times.

Her only concern was the rotting corpses in the large concrete water tank at the back of the property. If anyone opened the lid the stench would be undeniable. She didn't think he would have any reason to go back there. She should have disposed of the bodies before. But she wouldn't let that spoil such a wonderful day.

# CHAPTER 90

W hen Mei heard the news about May Simmons, she sighed with relief. Her fear Audrey Wetherby was back was keeping her awake at night. At Geoff's insistence, they had never mentioned the money they found under the old shed attached to the cottage to anyone, especially not the police. It was a lot of cash, almost $750,000. She presumed it belonged to Audrey. Who else would have hidden the money and never returned for it?

She remembered the day they found it. She had spent almost all of her dead husband's insurance money. Well, technically, although she always referred to him as her ex-husband, he actually he died before they were married, but she had been carrying his child at the time of his death, so she inherited all his assets, including his life insurance. Unfortunately, her little boy died just a few months after birth. It was his heart. He was so tiny. The only way she could deal with the grief was to put all her energy into converting the old Tiromoana Cabins into a multimillion-dollar five-star luxury resort. It took two years and a lot of money. She had needed Audrey's cash.

Mei's life in New Zealand had been a lonely one until she met Geoff. He grounded her. She knew he would do anything to protect her. She also knew that he was serious about shooting Audrey if ever she set foot on the property. Mei didn't know if this was to keep the money a secret or just doing his civil duty, but either way, she was glad Audrey was not responsible for the recent murders.

It was still raining. The gardens were in desperate need of it. Mei loved her gardens. She put on her raincoat and gumboots and went to check on her pride succulents. The reds, greens, yellows, and browns of her bromeliad collection brightened in the rain. She walked over to the garden by the outside restaurant she had planted over Audrey's tin box and paused awhile. Was she imagining it or had the plants been rearranged? Mei knew every plant she had planted, every bromeliad, every agave. Her heart stopped. They were different, she was sure of it. Geoff never touched the gardens, it wasn't his thing, but someone had. Surely not. She found she couldn't catch her breath. She had to know. She grabbed a spade from the nearby shed and began to remove the plants. One by one, she lay them gently on the ground and proceeded to dig. She wasn't exactly sure where the box had been. There was only one way to find out. She had to remove all the plants so she could know for sure.

"What the hell are you doing, girl?"

Mei looked up to see Geoff standing there looking at her in amazement.

"Don't you know it's raining?" he asked. Then he realized exactly what she was doing. He looked at the area, now just a big muddy wet hole, and he knew. His face fell. "She knows."

"It's gone." Mei wiped the rain from her face. "She is back, Geoff."

"Fuck the woman. We should have put surveillance lights out here. When the hell did she take it?"

"I weeded all the gardens just a couple of weeks ago. I would have noticed the plants had been rearranged."

Mei began to fill in the hole and return the plants to their original position. She was keeping busy, so she didn't have to think. What could they do? They couldn't tell the police because they would have to explain the money.

"We do nothing, we say nothing," Geoff said quietly.

Looking at him with wide eyes, Mei said, "She is back, Geoff. She murders people. She will know we took the money. I am scared."

# CHAPTER 91

J ohnny was enjoying his work at the villa. The company wasn't bad, either. He couldn't help noticing the way his employer looked at him. Like he was her next meal. It made him a little uncomfortable, but he had to admit it was flattering. She was a good-looking woman. A little while ago she had gone out in the old Ute. Said she was picking up some wine and beer. Suggested he join her when he finished his jobs today. He might just take her up on that.

Johnny climbed the ladder on the old villa to check the roof gutters. For the past two days rain had finally hit the far north. The gutters were filled with leaves. He grabbed a bucket and began to remove the debris. Rainwater was the only source of water for the villa; if the gutters were blocked, the water couldn't get into the tanks. Having cleared the gutters, he checked the pipes to the tanks. The rain was heavy, and he would be able to hear the water flowing into the large concrete structures. As he neared the two big concrete tanks on the side of the hill, he could smell it. Rotting flesh. Fuck! A possum or rats had got into a tank. He would have to reroute the water so it only flowed into one tank while he removed whatever had died. There was no doubt which tank the odor was coming from. Then he noticed someone had disconnected the pipe going into the tank.

He removed the concrete lid to find it was a quarter full. The stench was indescribable. The light was not good. He reached for his phone and shone the light into the tank. Holy shit! The bodies were swollen and fully clothed. Johnny had dealt with dead animals his whole life. He enjoyed pig hunting and had even worked at the freezing works when he was younger. But dead humans were another thing altogether. He shone the light onto one of the bodies and thought he recognized old Matt. *Fuck! If that is old Matt who is the other body?* His mind was racing. Was it his daughter, Kathy? How did they get into the tank? Who put them in the tank? Johnny was no fool. This was murder. He knew he was in a tight spot. He took a photo, closed the lid, and walked away.

The woman he knew as Kathy Lane was walking up the pathway carrying bags of shopping. "Here, let me help," he offered.

"That would be great. Can you grab the wine and beer out of the car?" she requested.

Johnny was in shock. Operating on auto mode. Who was the woman in the tank with old Matt? Who is this woman? He needed to call the police. Picking up the boxes of wine and beer, he followed her to the villa and put them down on the back step. He needed to get out there, now.

She smiled. "Thanks, Johnny, come in. I'll put on the kettle. You are drenched. What have you been doing outside in the rain?"

"Just checking the roof for leaks. Can I have a rain check on the coffee? I need to pick up some tools from my house."

"Oh, come on, you need a break. I picked up some

wonderful banana cake from the shop. I simply won't take no for an answer," she said, smiling.

Johnny felt trapped. Who was she? What was she doing with two dead bodies in her water tank? *Fuck! This is fucking unbelievable!* His heart was pounding, but he tried to appear calm. "Banana cake is my favorite," he replied.

# CHAPTER 92

Today there were only five new cases of Covid-19. All could be traced to existing cases. Jimmy Bromley was working on the government's new automated tracing system. It would be one of the best in the world. He was proud of what his government was doing. All political parties were working together to eradicate the virus. Five million New Zealanders were working together to keep the country safe. Unlike in the USA, where white supremacists were picketing on the streets demanding to go back to work. The number of deaths was continuing to grow worldwide with almost 165,000 deaths. Over 2.2 million had contracted the virus. Most countries had acted too late to contain the virus. Bromley was glad New Zealand had taken decisive action early.

His workload was increasing daily as they were increasing their testing abilities. They had tested almost 90,000 New Zealanders to date. They needed to test many more before they could get an accurate read on community transmission. So far there were only a handful of cases that had not been traced to an existing cluster.

He was pleased when he heard the Anna Ward and May Simmons case had been solved. He wasn't surprised they were the same person. At least he could trace where Martin had contracted the virus. They were still tracing the whereabouts of Anna Ward, aka May Simmons, since leaving Auckland Airport. Anyone she had been in contact with over the past four weeks. Poppy didn't believe she had killed herself; she was convinced the woman was still out there somewhere. He hoped she was wrong about that.

The fact that Audrey Wetherby had no role in the mystery was no surprise, either. But, on the other hand, he would have liked to put her behind bars where she belonged. Nothing would give him or Poppy more pleasure.

His phone buzzed with a message. "Call me!" It was from DC Mason.

# CHAPTER 93

Johnny Woods walked into the Mangonui police station and asked for DC Mason. He was told to wait; Mason would be back in the station shortly. He checked his phone. There was another message from her. "Where are you?" He didn't reply.

Finally, a man appeared. "Can I help you?" he asked.

"DC Mason? "Can I have a word with you?" Johnny asked.

"Follow me."

Johnny followed Mason into a small room at the back of the station.

"Have a seat. What can I do for you?"

His voice was nervous. "I have something to report. It's something I've found."

"Yes, what?"

"I am working for a woman in Totara North. Kathy Lane, she said her name was."

"Kathy Lane? I see."

"She hired me to work on the villa. Old Matt Lane's villa. She told me he passed away recently and wants to put it on the market."

"Go on."

"Well, this morning I was cleaning the leaves from the gutters and decided to check the pipes to the tanks. There was an awful smell coming from one of the tanks. When I lifted the lid, this is what I saw." He handed his phone to the detective.

"Jesus Christ! Is that what I think it is?" Mason asked.

"Yes, two bodies, and I'm pretty sure one is old Matt's. I think the other one may be his daughter, Kathy."

"Did you confront Kathy Lane about the bodies in her tank?"

"No. she was out when I found them. I never said a word. I was pretty much in shock. She has no idea I know they are there."

"So, you presume she knows they are in her water tank?"

"It's her father, for God's sake! She said he passed away recently. She didn't say he was in the fucking water tank. I figure she killed him, and the young woman, and now is selling their house."

DC Mason just sat staring at him. 'How long ago was this?"

"Must be a couple of hours now," he said, checking the time. "She arrived home just after I found them and insisted I join her for a coffee. I tried to make an excuse to leave, but she wasn't having it. So, I stayed and drank coffee and ate banana cake and nearly shit my trousers. I did do something, though." He dug into his pocket and produced a tissue in a plastic bag. "I thought you could run her DNA and check if she is Kathy Lane."

"This is her tissue?" Mason asked?

"Yes, I took it from the bin in the bathroom when I went in to wash my hands. The woman gives me the creeps. Oh yes, she's all smiles and looks perfect, but there is something that just isn't right. If she had suspected that I knew anything, I was pretty sure she would scarper, or worse, shoot me."

"So, she is there now, and the bodies are still in the tank?" Mason asked.

"She comes and goes quite a bit. I don't know. All I know is that she knows where I live and I'm guessing she murders people!" Johnny said.

DC Mason sat looking at the photo of two bloated bodies in the bottom of a water tank. The tank was only partly full, and the bodies were floating on the surface. It was a gruesome scene.

"So, will you arrest her?" Johnny asked.

DC Mason knew this was bigger than just a local Totara North woman with a couple of bodies in her water tank. He suspected this woman was tied to the other murders and to the missing Anna Ward, aka May Simmons, and possibly aka Kathy Lane. *Who is this woman?* he wondered. He was holding her DNA in his hand. He had his suspicions. He picked up the phone and called Jimmy Bromley. If anyone knew Audrey Wetherby, he did. She was his Achilles' heel.

# CHAPTER 94

Sirens pierced through the quiet late afternoon in the seaside village of Totara North. Residents emerged from houses, watching from front lawns and balconies as police cars streamed by in a continuous procession only to disappear around the corner by the jetty.

DC Mason, Constable Patterson, and their teams closed off the area around the villa as armed officers, a dog squad, and frontliners swarmed the property. After a thorough search of the villa they gave the all-clear. No one was found on the premises. The bodies were removed from the concrete water tank. A helicopter overhead was searching for the woman known as Kathy Lane.

Tracy Mason was first on the scene reporting for the local and national media. "Two bodies have been found in a water tank in the backyard of a property here in Totara North. At this time the bodies have not been identified but are believed to be local Totara North residents. A search is underway for the woman who has been living on the property and who the police think may be responsible for the murders. I have with me Johnny Woods, who

227

discovered the bodies while working on the property. Mr. Woods, I understand you found the bodies."

"Yes, awful sight. Wish I hadn't seen it."

"Did you recognize them?"

"The bodies were pretty disfigured. Looked as though they had been in the tank for a few days. The police said I cannot say any more. Sorry."

"This is the third body found here in the small fishing village of Totara North. Just recently, the body of a forty-five-year-old woman, Keke Green, was found in the harbor by the old sawmill. The police think there may also be a connection to two homicides that took place in Remuera four weeks ago. It would appear we have another serial killer in Northland. Only three years ago Audrey Wetherby disappeared, leaving in her wake a stream of murders from Whangaroa to Hihi. Is this another serial killer? Or could it be that Audrey Wetherby has returned to her familiar killing ground? This is Tracy Mason for Livestream News New Zealand."

# CHAPTER 95

As Audrey was driving north, emergency vehicles were driving south. Her instinct to leave the villa had been heightened by the sight of muddy footprints around the water tank. Bloody men! Taking her laptop and a quickly packed bag, she grabbed Matt's old raincoat, baseball cap, and a pair of Kathy's gumboots and headed to safety. She had fucked up, she knew it. All she wanted was to collect her cash and continue on living her life. What was wrong with that? She needed a drink, badly. She reached into her bag, removed a small bottle of Lindauer Brut, unscrewed the top, and drank. Thank God the old man had a collection of antiquated cars. Never in her wildest dreams did she think she would be driving an old rusty junk dressed like a vagabond and running from the law.

The rain was heavy and the windshield wipers were barely operating, making it difficult to see the Hihi turnoff. Water was accumulating on the camber of the road. The combination of lockdown and the rain was proving to be a godsend. No one was out walking Hihi Beach. The campgrounds were closed. A sad handwritten sign on the shop door confirmed it would be closed for some time. She passed Tiromoana Resort and continued up the winding gravel road until she came to an old track leading to an abandoned house. The owner had long departed the property. It smelled of damp carpet and dead rodents. The owner was an artist and had converted an old shed into a studio. She pushed open the barn door and stood surrounded by large kauri sculptures. Most had never been completed. Their shapes protruded from large stumps of old kauri trees, faces half-formed. Cobwebs hung from the rafters. It was a dire atmosphere, but it was the lesser of two evils. She placed her bag on an old workbench and opened a second bottle of champagne. Intermittent bursts of thunder could be heard in the distance. She was safe here. She had time to think.

# CHAPTER 96

J immy Bromley was allowed access to the scene at the villa. It was shocking. The bodies of Matt and Kathy Lane had been identified by the police. It left no doubt that the woman living in the villa claiming to be Kathy Lane was an imposter. They were waiting for the DNA results of the tissue that Johnny Woods had provided. It would be another forty-eight hours before they got the results. The police had wiped for fingerprints and gathered DNA from items left in the home but presumed they would belong to Matt and Kathy.

DC Mason asked Jimmy Bromley if he thought it possible that Audrey Wetherby was responsible for the murders. Bromley said there was no evidence that Audrey was back in the area. Unless they could come up with some proof she was back, they should presume this woman was acting alone and was possibly a copycat perpetrator. That said, he advised DC Mason to send someone to the Tiromoana Resort to check on the owners as a precaution.

Jimmy Bromley would have liked nothing better than to know Audrey was responsible for the current murders. He had never really forgiven himself for allowing her to escape justice. But no one could say they had seen her. If one woman was carrying out these murders, then she had come from California on AIRNZ1 almost five weeks ago. She had been infected with Covid-19 and had contaminated at least one known person, Martin Melrose. His death now would be reopened as a possible homicide. He was the only person who could identify the woman, May Simmons . . . or was he? If May Simmons had taken Kathy Lane's identity, then there may be one other person who could identify her. Poppy had told him that Kathy Lane had stayed a couple of nights at the Tiromoana Resort. That pretty much squashed the theory that Kathy Lane was Audrey Wetherby. Mei knew Audrey Wetherby and would have recognized her. Or would she? Had Audrey Wetherby changed her appearance? Could she change it that dramatically? Had she been hiding behind face masks, using the epidemic as a way to avoid detection? There was only one way to find out. Bromley needed to talk to Mei personally.

"I am off to Tiromoana in Hihi," he called out to DC Mason. "There is something I need to follow up."

# CHAPTER 97

Tracy, Poppy, and Rose had been trying to contact Mei for hours. There was no reply.

"Where the hell is she?" Rose said.

The women were concerned. They all lived within just a few miles of each other and made a decision to break the rules and meet at the Tiromoana Resort to check on Mei.

"We can all abide by social distancing. We can take our own cars and just check she is okay," Poppy said.

"No one will need to know. We can be there in twenty minutes and drive directly to her house. In this storm they might be out on the property checking the resort. A hundred acres is a big area to keep on top of. But I will feel a lot happier if I know Mei is okay," Tracy said.

Access to the resort was becoming precarious. Branches and debris were spewed across the gravel road. The three cars drove the long driveway to Mei's house at the end of the ridge overlooking the bay. The view across to the Karikari Peninsula was obscured by a white blanket of constant rain. It was not cold, with autumn mild temperatures. The women all ran from their cars to the shelter of the entranceway, ignoring social distancing as they stood huddled under the small awning. They rang the doorbell and heard the chime echoing inside. There was no response. Tracy ran around the side of the house and onto the decking that spanned three sides. She could see inside the open-plan kitchen, dining, and lounge area. "No one seems to be home," she called to them. "Rose, check the bedrooms on the other side."

There was no sign of Mei or Geoff.

"Let's head over to the resort," Poppy said. "Maybe they are working over there."

As they took the narrow access road to the resort, they saw a police car parked by the main office.

"Fuck!" Poppy said. "We're not supposed to be here."

"Too late now," said Tracy. "We might as well find out what's going on."

The police knew no more than they knew. Mei and Geoff were nowhere to be seen. They had checked the house, the chalets, the cabins, the sheds, and there was no sign of them. The policeman gave the women a warning. "You are not supposed to leave your home to visit a friend," he said sternly.

A car was coming up the driveway toward the resort. They all watched as it approached.

"'It's Jimmy," Poppy said.

"I was hoping it was Mei." Tracy was getting more concerned.

"They could just be out getting supplies," Rose said hopefully. "Should we wait?"

When Jimmy Bromley saw his wife and her merry band of sleuths, he suggested they leave. "They are most likely checking on the property in all this rain. I'll let you know when they return," he said.

The three women were hesitant to leave. "Promise," said Poppy. "As soon as you know anything, anything at all."

"Anything" he said.

# CHAPTER 98

It was day twenty-nine of lockdown at Alert Level 4. There were three new cases, but the figure stayed at 1,451 as three cases from yesterday were previously confirmed cases off a ship from Uruguay. Three new deaths, eight people in hospital and one in ICU, and still sixteen significant clusters.

Daily Covid-19 news reports at one o'clock had become part of New Zealand's lockdown way of life. Watching the number of new cases decrease daily was encouraging and rewarding for the five million New Zealanders who were sacrificing their freedom to stay home and stay safe. It was Anzac weekend this weekend. The police were setting up roadblocks into all holiday locations, the far north being no exception. After all, it was one of the most popular destinations for Aucklanders who had holiday homes in the seaside villages four hours north of the city.

DC Mason had his hands full. Hihi was in his jurisdiction and the disappearance of Mei Wong and her partner Geoff Gannon was a concern. Their cars were still in their garage. Strangely, their boat was missing, but no sign of them nor their boat had been seen. The coastguards had done a thorough search of the bay and had even gone out into the open sea to search for the couple to no avail.

Likewise, there were no sightings of the mystery woman who had taken over the identity of Kathy Lane and was wanted for a number of murders. The bodies of Kathy and Matt Lane had been autopsied and there was found to be a high quantity of oleander in their systems at the time of death. The police knew they definitely had a serial killer on their hands. She was about five foot four inches, black hair, slight build, and spoke in a quiet voice with an American–New Zealand mixed accent. She had used a number of aliases including Anna Ward, May Simmons, and Kathy Lane. DC Mason expected to get the DNA from the tissue today. He had asked to fast-track the information so he could determine who the woman was and if they had her DNA on record.

It was two in the afternoon before he received the phone call. The DNA from the tissue Johnny Woods had taken out of the bin in the bathroom belonged to the real Kathy Lane. She must have dropped it in the bin before she was killed. Also, the DNA taken from the document in Bruce Sutton's pocket only had his DNA on it. They were back to square one. It was frustrating.

But when DC Mason received a second phone call, everything changed.

# CHAPTER 99

Audrey finished her last bottle of champagne and felt surprising good. Under the old raincoat she was wearing a rather stunning outfit, compliments of Kathy's wardrobe. Cute jeans and soft flowing jacket. She had to admit Kathy had great taste. Her surroundings, however, did not suit her attire. She needed to find new living quarters, preferably with a stocked fridge and more bubbles. Audrey knew most of the homes up the peninsula were not occupied during lockdown. But finding one that had food would be more challenging. Her best choice was the multimillion dollar homestead at the top of the hill. The owners lived overseas. The property had been on the market for a long time. She presumed they would at least have a stocked wine cellar and hopefully a pantry. It was worth a shot.

She started up the old car and made her way up the road in the pouring rain, which was gouging deep holes in the gravel. The main gate to the property was bolted shut, but to her surprise, there was no padlock, so she simply opened the gate, entered the property, and closed the gate behind her.

Getting access to the house was not as easy. She was amazed

by the fact that there was no security system. She checked for cameras and signs of security paraphernalia and, finding none, she smashed a window in the laundry and climbed over the sill. The house was simply beautiful. A quick tour of the kitchen confirmed her faith in the rich and famous. The pantry had a nice stock of essentials and a collection of most suitable wines.

Audrey set about to make a nice meal using dried spaghetti, capers, and a can of Wattie's tinned tomatoes, complemented with a bottle of good New Zealand merlot. She wasn't really a red wine drinker, but what the hell, there was no champagne and this was a special occasion. It could be her last meal in the free world.

She wondered why she hadn't thought of staying here before, but really it was too risky. Rich people had other people who hired more people to watch over their assets. She figured it wouldn't be long before someone came to fluff the pillows, or water the plants, or mop the floors. She just needed a comfy bed for the night. She presumed there was no power in the house. She used the gas hob to cook her dinner and ate it by candlelight. The bed was all she hoped it to be. Audrey slept like she didn't have a worry in the world.

# CHAPTER 100

The six o'clock news covered the Northland murders. The police were looking for a woman of interest. She was last seen in Totara North. Searches were taking place in various seaside towns. Roadblocks were set up south of Kaeo all the way north to Kaitaia.

Jimmy and Poppy Bromley were watching from the comfort of their sofa. It had been a frustrating day. There had been no sign of Mei and Geoff and no success in locating the woman.

When Jimmy's phone rang, he saw it was DC Mason.

"Jimmy, you won't believe it. We have her. Audrey Wetherby's blood was found on the floor of old Luke Street's house in Totara North. I can't fucking believe it. We found a couple of drops of blood which were collected from the scene. Because we presumed the old man had simply died of booze and old age, they never bothered to test them. When the woman in the cottage confessed to the other murders, I asked to have them DNA tested. They came in positive for Audrey Wetherby. She is here, Jimmy. Audrey Wetherby is back in Northland," he said excitedly.

Jimmy was speechless. "What is it?" Poppy asked. "What did he say?"

"Audrey Wetherby's blood was found at Old Luke Street's place," he repeated. "What now?" he asked Mason.

"We find her," he replied. "This time we won't let her get away. The area is completely blocked off. No one can get in or out of the country without good reason. There is not much we can do tonight. The coastguard has searched the beaches and coves around the bay. Tomorrow they will do a more extensive search. We don't know if their disappearance is tied to Audrey Wetherby, but there is a good chance it is."

"I want to be there when you find her," said Jimmy.

"Anything you can do to help the search, we would be grateful. Talk tomorrow. Goodnight, Jimmy."

"I have got to tell the girls," Poppy said as she opened up her laptop. "This is big!"

# CHAPTER 101

Day thirty of lockdown brought out the sunshine and blue skies. Doubtless Bay was glistening in the morning light. Audrey woke to the sound of a helicopter buzzing over the peninsula. She checked the news to find that she was not the only one the police were looking for. Mei and Geoff were also missing. Yesterday she was so preoccupied with her own situation she had not given a thought to what was going on around her. So, they were looking for Mei and Geoff. Did they know she was in Hihi too? Surely not. Why would they be missing? It just didn't make sense.

Her laptop would run out of battery soon. She searched online for any information on her case to find they had set up roadblocks throughout the north hoping to prevent her from leaving the area. They said they had DNA linking her to Old Luke's murder. She remembered cutting her arm on the gorse bushes. *Damn!* she chastised herself. *Stupid mistake.*

She wouldn't be in this situation if it wasn't for bloody Mei stealing her money. She would have taken the money and moved on. At that moment she heard a key turn in the front door. *Fuck!*

"Who's here?" she heard a female voice call out from the front entranceway.

Audrey knew she had left her bag in full view on the kitchen table.

"Who are you?" She confronted the slender red-haired woman holding a suitcase.

"Helen Adams," she replied. "I own this property."

"Oh, Helen, I am so pleased to meet you," Audrey said sweetly. "I live just up the road. I was worried that no one was living here and with all the activity going on in the area I stopped by to check on the house. There has been a break-in. The window around the back has been broken. I can't see any damage. Have you just arrived here? How did you get here in lockdown?"

Audrey knew this woman was her gift. "Please let me show you the window."

The woman followed Audrey to the back of the house.

"I have been in quarantine," she said. "I was released this morning and told I could return home. I flew in from London and was put into a hotel in Auckland for the past two weeks."

"Do you have family here?" Audrey asked.

"No, I have no family. My parents both passed away recently in London. I used to live near here."

"This is a beautiful property," Audrey said. "You are going to love it here. Don't worry about the window, I'll have my husband pop over and fix it later this afternoon. You must be dying to see the house. Let me leave you to enjoy it."

"Thank you. What did you say your name is?" Helen asked.

Audrey walked over to her bag on the kitchen counter and removed a gun old Matt had unknowingly provided and shot the woman front and center.

Now Audrey had a plan.

# CHAPTER 102

The police were diligent in their search. Every cabin, chalet, and corner of the Tiromoana Resort was thoroughly checked for any sign of the missing owners and Audrey Wetherby. Helicopters had searched the densely covered bush areas of the peninsula and the coastguard was still searching the beaches and coves.

There was no sign of Northland's infamous serial killer. All roadblocks had been operating since late yesterday afternoon. There was no chance of Ms. Wetherby escaping authorities. The police had two photos they had distributed to all law enforcement: one slender with dark hair and one blonde and more buxom. She could look different again, they had been instructed. "Makes it bloody difficult to identify her, I know" said DC Mason. But check all IDs. You have all her aliases."

There were still no sightings of Mei and Geoff, which had Mason worried. He knew them well. Yes, their boat was gone. Had they known Audrey was back and taken off somewhere? Or had Audrey killed them too and absconded in their boat? *Where the fuck is she?*

The search had continued on into the early evening before it was called off. They would be back at daylight. They left a police presence at Mei's house in case Mei and Geoff returned.

Jimmy Bromley was so determined to find Audrey Wetherby, he said he would stay at the resort overnight in case she decided to come back. Mason thought it was a little obsessive but understood the man wouldn't rest until the woman was locked up for a long time.

As Mason drove out of the resort, he called his wife. "Trace, I'm heading home now. We found nothing. Jimmy Bromley is staying at the resort tonight in case something or someone turns up. See you soon, sweetheart."

# CHAPTER 103

The fire was intense. Flames leapt into the night sky. Its bright orange glow could be seen for miles. Every cabin, every chalet was ablaze. Flames had spread into the pine and eucalyptus forest bordering the property. The Hihi fire brigade was the first to arrive but all they could do was to try and extinguish the flames. Most buildings had already burned to the ground. More emergency vehicles arrived at the scene. The sight was horrendous. The fire chief was asking where the owners were. "Is anyone staying here?" he kept repeating over and over again. There was no answer. Nobody knew.

DC Mason heard about the situation on his radio and rushed to the scene. "Jimmy Bromley and a few frontliners were staying in the chalets," he told them. But he could see there was no way anyone could have escaped the fire.

It took most of the night to douse the flames. Helicopters dropped fire retardant from above while firemen from multiple fire stations in the north worked on putting out the fire on the ground.

By morning there was just smoldering embers and complete devastation.

"It has to be arson," said the fire chief. "The fire looks like it started in numerous locations. Bodies have been found in the ruins. A man's body and a women's body."

DC Martin presumed it was Jimmy Bromley who had died in the fire. No one had been able to contact him. Poppy was inconsolable. "She has killed my husband just like she killed my brother," she sobbed. "It was Audrey, I know it was her."

The police located all the frontliners who were staying at the resort; thankfully, they had been working night shift at Kaitaia Hospital. The woman's body was yet to be identified. The coroner had estimated the age of the woman in the fire to be in her late forties or possibly early fifties. This ruled out the body belonging to Mei. She was only in her early thirties. The forensic team advised that DNA extracted from burnt bone fragments may be highly degraded as they are prone to contamination with external DNA. They may never be able to determine the identity of the victim.

There was nothing at the scene left to identify the body. Had Audrey realized she was trapped? Had she come back to Tiromoana to get her final revenge? After a while it was just a process of elimination. No one fitting that description was missing. No one, that is, except for Audrey Wetherby. Later the police found an old gun in the ashes and learned it had belonged to old Matt Lane.

The day after the fire, Mei and Geoff returned. They had been staying at the end of the peninsula in a small, isolated bach Geoff owned. They had not seen the fire and had only heard about it that morning. Both were shocked. They were just thankful the house had escaped the fire unscathed. When Mei walked into her bedroom there was a note sitting on her dressing table. It was from Audrey.

My dear Mei,
I understand why you did it.
But every action has a reaction. Every decision has consequences.
Our resort has gone. Everything we both built I have now destroyed.
I have set my life on fire.
Maybe my sins can be cleansed by the flames
And my soul arise anew from the ashes.
Take care.
Audrey

# CHAPTER 104

She sat sipping red wine looking out at the bay. Her name was Helen Adams. She had dual passports: British and New Zealand. She had a strong British accent. Forty-eight years old. Short, red hair, green eyes, and petite. She owned a large hundred-acre property on the Hihi peninsula. The woman was a recluse, preferring her own company to that of others. Her garden was spectacular. When the pandemic was over, she would take a trip home to England. In the meantime, life was good. She heard the owners of the resort nearby had decided to sell and move out of the area.

The woman was listening to Radio New Zealand. There were only five new Covid-19 cases today, bringing the total of confirmed cases to 1,456. There were seventeen deaths to date. One thousand and ninety-five people had recovered. They would be moving into Level 3 in a few days.

New Zealand was the first country in the world to attempt to completely eradicate the virus. Would they succeed?

## THE END

# ALSO BY LEONIE MATEER

## THE AUDREY MURDERS – BOOK SERIES

*The Murder Suite* —Book One

*The Cabin by the Sea* — Book Two

*The Murder Trail* — Book Three

*Murder in the Family* — Book Four

*The Murder Trap* — Book Five

*Murder in Lockdown* — Book Six

*The Taupo Bay Killings* — Book Seven

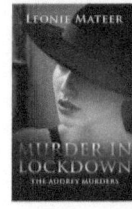 

If you enjoyed this book, I would be so appreciative if you would write a brief review on Amazon. Thank you.

Leonie Mateer

www.leoniemateer.com

# ABOUT THE AUTHOR

Puppeteer, children's entertainer, model agency owner, TV talk show panelist, luxury accommodation owner, entrepreneur, product developer, brand developer, storyteller, author, and indie publisher Leonie Mateer has lived a full and diverse life.

Born and raised in New Zealand, Mateer moved to the United States in her thirties to pursue business opportunities. She returned to New Zealand for several years in the 2000s, running a luxury lodge in Northland—which has been an inspiration for her crime series—and now splits her time between Northland, New Zealand, and the United States.

Mateer is known for her huge success as a brand development expert. She received 'Who's Who' awards from both Leading American Executives and American Inventors in the 1990s. As the creator of the brand Caboodles™, a teen girl brand that took the retail industry by storm in the late 1980s and early 1990s, she created a new retail category—the cosmetics organizer category —with Caboodles' global retail sales exceeding US$100 million worldwide.

Ms. Mateer also works in the real estate industry, specializing in residential and lifestyle properties in New Zealand's winterless far north.

Her two daughters and four grandsons live in the United States and are a constant inspiration for many of her stories.

## Other titles by Leonie Mateer:

### Business:

*The Caboodles Blueprint – Turn Your Idea into Millions*

*Have a Product Idea? – How Many Could You Sell?* – a collection of business articles.

### Health and wellbeing:

*Psoriasis – The Simple Cure – Who Knew?*

*Psoriasis - Staying Clear - The Healthy Alternative* – a must read for any psoriasis sufferer.

### Fiction:

"The Audrey Murders" – a seven book series starring Audrey Wetherby, a serial killer living in idyllic small towns in New Zealand.

### Children's fiction:

*The Magical World of Dantonia*

*Black Lake*

*The Bird Boys*

*Mason's Secret*

### Tarot Card Online Game

www.readyourownfortune.com

A do-it-yourself game that enables players to read their own fortunes online, anytime, anywhere. Her sixty-three-card deck, based on ancient fortune telling cards, has been deciphered with the assistance of professional psychics.